A Winter Love Story

Soft little snowflakes fell all around them, dusting their faces and clothing. Davey leaned over and took her face in his hands and turned it up toward him. "You look pretty in the moonlight," he said.

"That's reflected light from the lodge," Jessica answered but she let her face stay tilted upward, ready for his kiss.

Davey's lips pressed against hers as softly as butterfly wings and then he kissed her eyelids, her cheeks, and her nose. Once more, he kissed her mouth. This time it was a long, lingering kiss that told her what she already knew. But she wanted to hear it from him. "What was that for?" she asked.

Point Romance

A Winter Love Story

Jane Claypool Miner

Illustrated by Derek Brazell

■ SCHOLASTIC

Scholastic Children's Books,
Scholastic Publications Ltd,
7-9 Pratt Street, London NW1 0AE, UK

Scholastic Inc.,
555 Broadway, New York, NY 10012-3999, USA

Scholastic Canada Ltd,
123 Newkirk Road, Richmond Hill,
Ontario, Canada L4C 3G5

Ashton Scholastic Pty Ltd,
PO Box 579, Gosford, New South Wales,
Australia

Ashton Scholastic Ltd,
Private Bag 92801, Penrose, Auckland,
New Zealand

First published in the US by Scholastic Inc., 1993
First published in the UK by Scholastic Publications Ltd, 1994
Copyright © Jane Claypool Miner, 1993
Cover artwork copyright © Derek Brazell, 1994

ISBN: 0 590 55689 4

Printed by Cox & Wyman Ltd, Reading, Berks

Chapter 1

Friday

Cee Cee Davis and Tonya Jackson stood on the sidewalk outside the bus terminal and looked anxiously at every car that turned the corner. Cee Cee looked at her watch. "You'd think they could be on time. We've planned this skiing trip for ten months."

"They'll be here," Tonya said.

"Lauren will," Cee Cee agreed. "But when I talked to Jessica this morning, her mother was still fighting the idea."

"Jessica won't let her mother spoil this trip," Tonya said. "We've saved and planned for months. Her mother *promised*."

"Yes, but she never liked the idea." Cee Cee was worried. "Remember all that stuff about how sixteen is too young to travel alone and four girls could get in a lot of trouble at a ski lodge?"

"I remember," Tonya answered as she

breathed in the deep, cold air and exhaled a smoky fog of frost. "But Jessica's mom didn't put up any bigger fight than *my* parents did. Or for that matter, than your mom did."

"Only Lauren's folks really wanted her to go," Cee Cee agreed. "They were so busy worrying about her broken heart that they probably would have agreed to a trip to Squaw Valley."

"Squaw Valley?" Tonya laughed. "Going to Mount Paradise isn't like going to Idaho. We're only taking a four-hour bus ride from Connecticut."

"I hope we *do* get into a lot of trouble," Cee Cee said. "Boy trouble. I hope there are lots and lots of wonderful men there."

Tonya looked at Cee Cee with understanding. She knew Cee Cee's father had deserted his family when Cee Cee was four years old. Tonya personally thought Cee Cee had been looking for "a man of her own" ever since.

Tonya shook her head and smiled at Cee Cee. "Don't count on lots of boys. Mount Paradise is a small family resort, not Aspen."

Before Cee Cee could answer, Lauren's family van turned the corner and Cee Cee breathed a sigh of relief. "One down," she said, "and three minutes till blast off. Jessica, where are you?"

Tonya watched as Lauren's father helped his daughter with her ski gear. Lauren Anderson was the only one who owned her own skis. Her dad took them off the top of the car and carried them over to the side of the bus where he stowed them in the open storage bins. Lauren carried her own bag and put that beside the others. Tonya noticed that Lauren and her father were almost the same height. Lauren must have grown another inch this year.

Her father kissed her on the cheek and said, "Be a good girl."

"Daddy!" Lauren protested.

Mr. Anderson frowned and said, "Be sure and tell the truth about your age, honey. You're only sixteen and make sure people know it." Then he turned to his daughter's friends and said, "Merry Christmas, girls."

"Merry Christmas," Tonya answered. "Don't worry about Lauren, we'll have a great time."

"I know *you* are a sensible girl," he said to Tonya and his glance indicated that he wasn't so sure about his own daughter or Cee Cee. "Just stick together and watch out for each other. You know, use the buddy system. On and off the slopes."

Tonya flashed Mr. Anderson her most reassuring smile. She didn't blame him for worrying about Lauren — not because she was reckless but because Lauren looked like a glamorous young woman instead of a teenage kid — at least from a distance.

"Get aboard," the bus driver called out.

"Merry Christmas," Mr. Anderson repeated and kissed Lauren before he got into his van and drove away. Once again the bus driver called out for them to board. The girls pretended they didn't hear him.

"Where's Jessica?" Lauren asked.

"Late," Tonya answered. "Cee Cee thinks she may not be able to come after all."

"I'll die," Cee Cee promised. "I'll simply die if Jessica doesn't come with us. Jessica is the glue."

Tonya shook her head. "No, you're the glue, Cee Cee. You just don't know it."

Lauren nodded her head gravely. "That's right, Cee Cee. We all met *you* first."

"Sure, in the sixth grade," Cee Cee laughed. "That was five years ago. I may be the instigator of this snow bunny trip, but . . ."

"Girl, you're *not* going to call us snow bunnies all week, are you?" Tonya interrupted. "I'm too liberated to be any kind of bunny."

"Well, I hope you won't be *too* liberated this week," Cee Cee cautioned her friend. "We're going to have a wonderful, romantic vacation and we should enjoy it."

"I just hope there won't be so much ice that the skiing is bad," Lauren said.

Her two friends fell silent, recognizing that Lauren obviously didn't want to talk about romance. Tonya felt sorry for her as she saw that Lauren's eyes were red and she was staring a long way into space again. Tonya wished that Lauren would hurry up and get over her breakup with Brian. It had happened at Thanksgiving and here it was Christmas Day. Just because you had been going together for two years didn't mean you had to stay in mourning forever. Or did it? Tonya had to admit she had no experience with love. A crush maybe, but not love.

The bus driver honked and leaned out the door to yell, "You girls coming or not?"

"What should we do?" Cee Cee asked.

"Stall," Tonya answered. "Lauren, you go talk to him."

"Flirt," Cee Cee ordered. "It will be good practice."

Lauren looked appalled at the idea of flirting with the middle-aged, grumpy bus driver. She didn't protest but she didn't move, either. She asked, "Do you think Jessica really might not come?"

"Jessica was determined," Cee Cee answered in a worried voice.

"Well, we can't wait long," Tonya said grimly. "He's pulling out."

The three girls watched as the bus driver made a show of shutting the door and backing the bus up about two feet. Before they had to decide whether or not to make a run for the bus, Jessica Mitchell's car pulled around the corner.

"Great!" Cee Cee said. "I'll start boarding and he'll have to wait for her." She went to the bus and pounded on the door. As the bus driver opened the door, she made a great pretense of dropping her bag and then moving slowly up the steps.

Tonya and Lauren inched toward the bus, watching as the Mitchells' car maneuvered into a parking place. Ms. Mitchell got out of the car with Jessica and followed her to the bus. Tonya could tell that there had been a big battle at the last minute.

Jessica looked cheerful and happy, as she always did. With her slim body and her soft, light brown hair, Jessica was one of those girls who seemed ordinary when you first met her. But when you really looked at her, she was pretty, and she was one of the most popular girls in Hoover High School.

Tonya thought Jessica looked especially attractive this afternoon. She had bright pink cheeks, probably from the heater in the car, and the lavender-blue knitted scarf she wore around her neck made her eyes look deeper and bluer. Yet, Tonya knew that compared to her own warm brown skin, high cheekbones, and black hair, Jessica wasn't a standout. Cee Cee's bright red hair and cute personality attracted a lot of attention, too. Of course, none of them compared to Lauren.

Tonya turned to look at Lauren who was moving toward the bus. She must be close to six feet now, Tonya thought, and every inch is gorgeous. Lauren's soft blonde hair fell to her shoulders. She wore a black ski jacket with turquoise diagonal stripes over the shoulders and loose black pants.

Jessica sounded relaxed as she called out, "Sorry I'm late." Then she turned to her mother and said, "I'll take those bags now, Mother," in a very firm voice.

Ms. Mitchell held onto the bags and said, "I'll give them to the bus driver. You shouldn't be lifting things."

"Mother . . ."

"Well, it's true, Jessica." Then she turned to Tonya and said, "I want you to watch Jessica. She shouldn't overdo on the slopes. Will you promise me?"

Tonya nodded her head and said, "I promise, Ms. Mitchell. We'll take good care of Jessica."

Jessica kissed her mother on both cheeks, took her by the shoulders, then gently turned her toward the car. " 'Bye, Mom, don't worry."

But her mother stood her ground and turned back and said in a shrill voice, "Don't treat me like a child, Jessica. *I'm* not the child, and I'm not being irrational about this. You know as well as I do that you shouldn't be going on this trip."

"I'm *going*, Mother," Jessica answered firmly.

"You shouldn't be going, and I've got half a mind to tell . . ."

"That's enough, Mother," Jessica said firmly. She took Ms. Mitchell by the arm and gently but firmly pulled her toward the car. Lauren and Tonya boarded the bus and by the time they were seated, they could see Jessica and her mother were still arguing. The three girls held their breath until their friend finally walked away from her mother and got on the bus.

As Jessica joined the three others in the

back of the bus, Cee Cee asked, "What was that all about?"

"Who knows?" Jessica answered shortly and then she added, "I'm kind of sleepy. Mind if I move over there and stretch out?" Before anyone could object, Jessica lay down on an empty seat and closed her eyes, shutting out her friends, and whatever the problem had been with her mother.

The bus was driving through town now and Tonya watched the Christmas lights flicker in the late afternoon darkness. She hoped the trip was a success but she really wondered if it would be. They had saved so hard, planned so long, and now things looked grim. Cee Cee, who was building big dreams about romance, was bound to be disappointed. Lauren was nursing a broken heart and was not a lot of fun anywhere, anymore. And now Jessica — good old reliable Jessica — seemed to be having some mysterious trouble.

Tonya sighed and turned her face toward the window to watch the last of the twinkling lights before they drove onto the highway. She wished with all her heart that this trip with her very best friends would turn out well. It would be something to remember when she moved to Washington, D.C., in two weeks. And in that exact moment, she decided that she definitely would not tell anyone about her father's appointment to the new president's cabinet until they came home. It was just good sense to put the news off. Why spoil the trip? The girls would be as heartbroken at her leaving them as she was. So she would keep the bad news to herself for a week longer. At least she wouldn't be the one who was responsible for spoiling their "dream trip."

Chapter 2

Jessica lay with her eyes closed, pretending to nap. As the bus rolled along the highway, it seemed to be singing a song to her but the words she heard weren't exactly a lullaby. *'Bye, 'bye, you're going to die.*

It was silly to be feeling such things, Jessica reminded herself. There was still a good chance that the new X rays would come in with a different verdict. Hadn't Dr. Whitaker said there was a possibility that the spot that showed up on the first film was simply a mistake? Jessica forced herself to breathe slowly and reminded herself of his advice. "Take it a day at a time, Jessica," he'd said. "With the labs closing over Christmas, there's simply no way to get the second results any sooner than Monday afternoon."

So she'd forced her mother and father to let her come on this trip, promising that she would come home Monday night if the new results really confirmed the worst. Today was Friday so that meant she had to find some way to get through three nights and days without letting her friends know what she was facing. It also meant she, too, had to get through the days.

Jessica kept her eyes closed, keeping back tears as she went over the details of the last two weeks. The first indication that something was wrong was when she'd climbed on a chair in the kitchen to help her mother get the best dishes down for Christmas dinner. She still wasn't sure what happened but she fell and she and the huge gold-rimmed platter came tumbling down onto the floor. When she came to, there was broken china and blood all over.

Her mother was screaming and Jessica was so busy trying to get her mother to calm down that she was amazed when the paramedics rang the bell. Her mother at least had had enough sense to call them. Jessica let them in and they put her on a stretcher and carried her to the ambulance. But the paramedics ended up spending more of their time and attention on Ms. Mitchell, who was so distraught that she had to have a shot the minute she got into the doctor's office.

Jessica was embarrassed by her mother's hysteria and she didn't enjoy getting her arm stitched, but she was more worried about her mother than anything else.

The doctor wanted to call Mr. Mitchell but Jessica talked him out of it because her dad was a trial lawyer and had an appearance in court that day. There was a pretty clear rule about interfering with court days. You simply didn't do it.

Anyway, Jessica hadn't been really worried about herself until Dr. Whitaker started asking all those questions. Somehow, his tone of voice told her he was looking for a reason for the tumble — something more than awkwardness or absentmindedness.

"So you blacked out," he said. "Was there a warning signal before?"

"No warning," Jessica said. "I'm not even sure I blacked out. Maybe I just stepped back or something."

"Dizziness?"

"No."

"You were fine and then you fell," Dr. Whitaker summarized as he took off his glasses and began to clean them with a tissue. Then he asked her mother to come in from the waiting room and wrote out an order for X rays. "Nothing to worry about," he assured Ms. Mitchell and it was those words which sent a chill down Jessica's spine. Somehow, the way he'd said them told her he was very, very worried.

So when the X rays came back, she wasn't as surprised as she might have been when he said there was an indication of trouble. She sat quietly in the chair, almost not breathing as Dr. Whitaker droned on and on about "the possibilities we are facing."

Finally, he'd said the words *brain tumor* and her mother had begun to sob. He'd turned from her mother then, almost as if he couldn't bear to see and hear her pain and he'd continued to talk to Jessica, explaining about going to Hartford to have an examination in a new, more precise kind of X-ray machine called an MRI on Tuesday.

"It's sort of like a big tube or a small submarine," Dr. Whitaker tried to joke, but no one laughed.

On the way out of the office, Dr. Whitaker patted her arm and said, "Not to worry yet. Let's take this a day at a time, shall we?"

Well, Jessica tried to take it a day at a time but her mother's fear was so strong that she felt as though she was being suffocated. It was hard enough to keep her own spirits up, but keeping her mother on track was almost too much for her. Finally, it had become so difficult to talk to her mother that Jessica begged her father to take the day off and go to Hartford with her for the MRI. The idea of making that long drive with her mother trying to choke back sobs while she maneuvered the highway traffic was more than Jessica could face.

Her father seemed to understand because he had taken the day off even though he was scheduled for court. For the first time in her life, Jessica had been glad that her father was such a silent man. The ride to the hospital was gloomy, she supposed, but at least it had been quiet.

As she lay down on the long metal stretcher, her father stood beside her. He held her hand until the stretcher began to move. As she slipped into the MRI tube, which really *did* look like a small submarine, Jessica's whole attention was on not showing how scared she felt. Her father's face was white and drawn and he looked twenty years older than usual.

As they put her in, she closed her eyes and tried to pretend she was in her own bed in her own room. But this was different, more closed-in darkness than sleep. This was more like death —

"Breathe deeply," Jessica said aloud. "Concentrate on your breathing. You'll be out of here soon."

Her father was right there when they

brought her out, looking anxiously down at her as he asked, "Did it hurt?"

"Not at all," Jessica answered. "It was just like they promised. A little noise, and nothing else. If I'd been more relaxed, I could have taken a nap." She didn't tell him about the panic she'd felt inside the dark machine. She didn't tell him that thoughts of death almost overwhelmed her until she forced herself to do the diaphragmatic breathing she'd learned in gym class.

Now, she felt as though she'd been through the worst of it. She was getting used to it. There was a possibility that she might have a brain tumor. There was even a possibility that she might die, but there was also a possibility that there was nothing wrong at all. She was tired of having gloomy thoughts hang like low clouds over her every move.

She'd fought like a tiger to go on this skiing trip because she genuinely hoped to have a good time. She would keep her problems to herself and have fun if it killed her. At that thought, Jessica smiled to herself.

Cee Cee said, "You're not sleeping, you're smiling," and threw an orange at Jessica. "Wake up and snack."

Jessica sat up and forced herself to really smile. She picked the orange up off her lap and began to peel it carefully, pulling the rind off in a petal pattern. When the orange was peeled, she popped one section into her mouth and let the juice flow along her tongue, enjoying the sweetness. Might as well enjoy life to the fullest, she reminded herself. Live a day at a time.

"What are you thinking?" Cee Cee demanded.

"I'm not thinking," Jessica answered, "I'm eating an orange."

"You're thinking," Cee Cee accused. "No thinking on our holiday. It's against the rules."

"Your mom sounded really worried," Tonya said. "What's up?"

"I had that fall and then the flu, remember?" Jessica kept her voice light. She had told everyone at school that she missed classes because of the flu. The last thing she'd wanted was a whole lot of sympathy or curiosity over what would probably turn out to be nothing. "And she never wanted me to leave on Christmas Day."

"My folks were upset, too," Lauren added. "They said they wanted me to go but my dad kept telling me to be careful."

"And use the buddy system," Cee Cee added. "I bet I find my buddy first."

Lauren nodded. "You probably will."

". . . Not," Cee Cee said cheerfully.

Tonya turned to Lauren and said, "Your dad did sound worried."

Lauren lowered her head and said in a half-mumble. "It's the phone calls. I've been getting a lot of phone calls from boys, and my dad doesn't approve."

Cee Cee laughed and said, "Well, he'd better get used to it. Now that you and Brian are busted up, you'll probably get phone calls from every guy in school."

"I hope just the tall ones," Jessica said. "That will leave some hope for the rest of us."

But Cee Cee was right, Jessica decided. Lauren would have plenty of calls. She grew more stunning each day. She was almost six feet tall, with long legs and a slender model's figure. And she had that long, blonde hair, and those gray-green cat's eyes with dark brows and lashes, and wide cheekbones.

"Maybe we could use you as bait," Cee Cee suggested. "Set you up on a pedestal and then slip them a small redheaded replacement."

Lauren looked so genuinely worried that all three of her friends laughed. Tonya reached out and patted Lauren's arm, saying, "Don't worry, girl. Cee Cee is only kidding."

"I'm not kidding," Cee Cee insisted. "I'm just thinking. What's the best way for us to meet men fast? Send the one with the long, yellow hair on ahead. Right?"

Tonya laughed. "*I* have no intention of playing silly games to fit into *your* romantic adolescent fantasies."

"Oh, you'll do fine, as is," Cee Cee assured her. "Just remember, this is a week of excitement, romance, adventure . . ."

"And skiing," Tonya reminded her. "Remember, we're going on a skiing holiday."

"Speak for yourself," Cee Cee said. "*I'm* going on a romantic holiday where I expect to meet Mr. Right. In fact, I may meet two or three Mr. Rights before the week is over. I know all about these ski lodges. They're filled with gorgeous guys, and I'm going to have at least one of them. Maybe half a dozen."

Lauren obviously wanted to change the subject. "I'm glad you're here, Jessica. It wouldn't have been the same trip without you."

Jessica smiled. "There was no way that I would miss it. This is the highlight of our junior year," she stopped because she was afraid they might hear the catch in her voice as she held back the sadness.

"Next year we'll be seniors," Cee Cee said, "and we'll plan an even greater trip — maybe Aspen."

"We'll all be looking for colleges," Lauren

reminded her. "Our folks may not let us take any extra trips."

Tonya sat quietly, not joining into the conversation about the future. She would be in Washington, D.C.

Jessica wanted with all her heart to stop talking about next year. At this point, she wasn't willing to think beyond next Monday. Who knew what her future held?

Chapter 3

Lauren looked out of her window at the trees covered with shimmering ice. The way the headlights of oncoming traffic hit the ice and reflected back, made her think of Thanksgiving Eve when she and Brian had sat on the top of "their hill" and watched the headlights together. That was the night he'd spoken the words she dreaded hearing. "I'm sorry, Lauren, but it has to be over between us."

"Why?" she'd asked, but she already knew that he'd been staring at the new girl in their Spanish class for weeks.

"Two years is a long time," he'd answered. "I'll be going off to college in the fall."

"But we have till then," she'd breathed softly, knowing that no matter what reasons he gave her, the real reason was Anne Pauling. Sweet Anne with her short curly black hair and bright smile. She didn't blame her for wanting

Brian. Anne was from California and lonely and Brian was a wonderful person.

As she thought about Brian, she stared out into the night. What would she do without him? They'd broken up the night before Thanksgiving and she'd cried all four days of vacation. That Monday, she'd seen Brian and Anne holding hands in the hall and she'd gone home from school sick. Since then, she'd tried to avoid seeing them. She was keeping up her grades and getting through the days, but that was all.

Brian, how could you? she asked silently for the thousandth time. She never got any answers. Perhaps there really wasn't an answer.

Tonya breathed on the window and rubbed a clean hole to look out of. She said, "It's really beautiful, isn't it?"

The shimmering icicles on the trees seemed to speed by them. Cee Cee said, "Yeah, ice. I hope there isn't any ice at Mount Paradise."

Lauren kept looking out the window so she wouldn't have to talk. She could sit there and pretend that the breakup had never happened; she could just enjoy the silver wonderland. The soft glow of the landscape was beautiful and it was good to be going far away from Brian and Anne. She was beginning to feel almost comfortable, and her fear about going to the ski lodge, without Brian, began to melt a little bit.

She began to breathe more regularly and more deeply and thought to herself, Maybe this trip really will be wonderful. Maybe it will be the high point of my life, as Cee Cee keeps promising. Maybe this will be the best trip I've ever taken.

Lauren had agreed to go because she loved to ski. When she was younger, each winter, she and her family had gone skiing several times. Her mother and father were both of Norwegian descent, and they had grown up in Minnesota, so they loved winter sports. Then, her mother died when she was ten and her father never set foot on the slopes again.

But she had skied a lot the last two years. Brian's family owned a house in Maine and she'd spent long weekends there with Brian, his parents, and his younger twin brothers and older sister. She wondered if Brian was taking Anne there this vacation. Then she shook her head and promised herself not to think about Brian. The purpose of this trip was to *forget* about him.

Lauren said to Cee Cee, "I'll teach you how to ski so you can really have some fun." She knew Jessica and Tonya were pretty good skiers, but Cee Cee had only been skiing a few times at Butternut Basin in southern Massachusetts.

"No, thanks," Cee Cee answered. "I'm going to find my own private ski instructor. Maybe six feet two, with blond hair and a Norwegian accent. Like this guy." She held up a magazine she had been looking at and asked, "What do you think?"

Lauren laughed and said, "I think you're funny."

"Funny as in odd? Or amusing?" Cee Cee asked.

"Amusing," Lauren assured her. "I wish I had your . . . your enthusiasm."

Cee Cee made a face. "I wish I could be as glamorous as you are."

"I'm not glamorous," Lauren protested.

"The important thing is you *look* glamorous," Cee Cee said.

"I'm going on this trip," Lauren said, "to ski!" But even as she said it, she wondered if she'd even enjoy skiing without Brian. And what would it be like to be in a real lodge instead of Brian's home? She remembered when she had been to Mount Paradise as a child that the social activities in the evening seemed magical and mysterious, with young men and women in brightly colored sweaters always laughing and flirting. She couldn't imagine being a part of that scene.

Lauren looked outside as the last rays of

the sun disappeared. She said to herself, I'm scared. There's no other way to say it. I'm really scared.

Just then, Cee Cee stood up and began strumming an imaginary guitar and singing to her friends. As she sang, she did a little dance, swaying back and forth with the motion of the bus. She was halfway through her act when the bus driver spoke over the loudspeaker, threatening to put her off the bus if she didn't sit down. She sat down.

Undaunted, Cee Cee said, "Let's make a deal right now, if we find a cute guy, we go for him. And the others leave him alone. Right?"

"Right," Lauren agreed promptly. Cee Cee could have every man in the place for all she cared. And like Tonya, she understood what motivated Cee Cee.

Tonya shook her head and asked, "Don't you ever think about anything but guys? How did you manage to make the honor society?"

"I only made the honor society one year and that was because Brice Marston was the president. He was great!"

Tonya shook her head and smiled. She would miss Cee Cee the most, just because Cee Cee was Cee Cee, she supposed.

Cee Cee was giving a lecture now on how

to behave, ". . . and so when this cute guy asks you if you want to go to the hot tub with him, you say, 'Oh, but I can't swim.' If he asks you if you want to go skiing with him, you say, 'Oh, I'd just love to. Will you carry my skis?' The whole idea is to give the boy the opportunity to wait on you hand and foot."

Cee Cee went on, "Of course, with Lauren it'll be different. She'll have to use her skis like clubs to keep them away from her."

Tonya reached up and shook Cee Cee's arm as a warning.

Cee Cee went on stubbornly, "The only reason I'll watch out for Lauren is . . . well, wherever Lauren goes she'll be the belle of the ball."

Lauren smiled wistfully and answered, "And wherever you go, Cee Cee, you'll be having all of the fun."

Cee Cee looked startled at that suggestion and then said, "You know, you may be right."

Chapter 4

It seemed to Tonya that they'd been on the bus for days and yet her watch told her it was only two and a half hours since they'd left Danbury. She said, "Cee Cee, if you're finished with that magazine, I'd like to look at the clothes."

"It's mostly swimsuits," Cee Cee said. "I hope you all brought yours."

"Yes, of course we did," the girls chimed in.

"Well, I hope you brought more than one, because it's at the spa where all the partying starts."

Tonya laughed at her friend and said, "To hear you tell it, we'll meet cute guys at breakfast, lunch, and dinner, on the slopes, and in the hot tub. I'll be surprised if we get into the ladies' rest room without meeting a cute guy there."

"Well, you've got to expect the best," Cee Cee announced easily. She moved to an empty seat and stretched out her legs. She was wearing her new Day-Glo orange-and-pink print jacket and hot-pink tights. Her boots were also pink and they had orange tassels on the tops. It was always easy to find Cee Cee because she had on the brightest clothes.

About then they pulled into a gas station with a small store attached. "Rest stop," the driver announced. "You have five minutes here."

All of the girls got up to stretch their legs. They noticed that the other two passengers took their suitcases with them and that they seemed to be leaving. "Guess we're going to have the bus to ourselves from now on," Tonya observed.

The small country store had a counter with six stools and the rest of the place was jammed full of souvenirs like maple syrup, aprons, postcards, and other junk that no one would want. The girls walked up and down the tight little aisles, trying not to knock the ceramic mugs over. As they wandered about, the bus driver drank a cup of coffee and Cee Cee walked over to the cash register, where a young man was reading a surfing magazine.

She said, "Hi, do you live here?"

The young man smiled at her and said, "Sure, Red. I was born here and lived here all of my life."

"This must be a *darling* town to live in," Cee Cee said.

The boy asked, "Where are you girls going?"

"Up to Mount Paradise."

"Oh yeah, that's nice," the boy said. "But why don't you stay right here for the week? We've got some little cabins right out back, and we can have a good time."

"But there's not much snow," Cee Cee answered. She backed off slightly. This was more than she'd bargained for. Tonya and Jessica smiled at each other as they watched her get out of this spot.

"Oh, it'll snow in a day or two," the boy said, "and in the meantime we can go into the city and go to the movies and ride around on my tractor. You could help me work in the store, and all kinds of things."

Cee Cee seemed torn between being delighted to have made such an easy conquest and scared of what he would suggest next.

When the bus driver stood up and said, "Come on, girls. Let's go," they all followed him except Cee Cee.

The bus driver started the motor and Tonya

called out, "Wait a minute! Our friend is still in there."

"She's had the same five minutes," the bus driver growled. "If she can't get back in time, too bad for her."

"Oh, please," Lauren begged the bus driver. "Let me go get her."

The bus driver shrugged and said, "Okay, but hurry up or I'll leave you both behind."

Lauren jumped down off the bus and ran into the cafe where Cee Cee was leaning with one elbow on the cash register, smiling at the young man. Lauren grabbed Cee Cee's jacket sleeve and started tugging. "Hurry up! We're going to be left behind!"

Cee Cee waved and laughed and said, "Okay, Charlie, I'll see you on the way back from Mount Paradise."

When they reboarded, the bus driver looked fiercely angry as he said, "Shouldn't have let you girls off at all."

"Sorry," Cee Cee said and smiled her sweetest smile. "We just got to talking."

"Yeah," the bus driver said. "Now sit down and behave yourselves . . . and you shouldn't talk to strangers."

Back in her seat, Jessica looked at her watch and said, "Gee, it feels like it's really late, but it's only five minutes till five."

"We'll be there at six," Cee Cee announced, "and the coffee shop is open till eight. But I'm going to skip dinner and go straight into the spa."

Tonya shook her head from side to side and said, "Girl, you're incorrigible."

Cee Cee answered smartly, "Just enthusiastic."

Chapter 5

"Okay, girls, we're here," the bus driver called out. "Get a move on."

They gathered up their things and moved quickly out of the bus onto the street of a very small town. "Wow!" Cee Cee said. "The brochure said the village was small but this is ridiculous." They were standing on the sidewalk in front of a diner and there were several small stores lining both sides of the street for about three blocks. There was one clothing shop, one record store, and nearly everything else seemed to be antique stores.

No one was on the street at all, and there were only a couple of cars parked about half a block down from the diner. Although the diner and the stores all had Christmas lights in their windows, the general effect was lonely and sad.

It was only six o'clock but it was bitter cold,

and the wind blew into the small spaces between their gloves and the sleeves of their jackets, and most of all, their faces and heads were cold.

Jessica pulled her light-blue knitted scarf up to cover her head as she asked, "How do we get to the Mount Paradise Lodge?"

"Call a cab." The bus driver pointed to a telephone inside the diner. The diner was locked tight.

"Our bus tickets say Mount Paradise Lodge," Tonya protested. "You're supposed to take us all the way."

"Too much ice on the road," he answered briefly. "When the road is icy, you have to take a cab."

"If our tickets say Mount Paradise Lodge, you should take us there," Tonya insisted quietly. "There doesn't seem to be much ice on the road to me."

"You aren't driving," the bus driver answered shortly.

"I understand that," Tonya said, "but there isn't any taxi around and it is very cold. I don't think your company, or the lodge, wants you to leave four young women to freeze on Christmas night, do you?"

The bus driver looked angry as he gazed up and down the empty streets of the village.

Then he shook his head and said, "Climb in. I'll drive you up."

The girls thanked him profusely and got back on the bus. This time, they sat up front with all their gear and the bus driver asked, "How come your folks let you go away on Christmas Day anyway?"

"We just celebrated a little earlier than usual," Jessica answered. "Had dinner at one o'clock instead of three."

"I've had to work every Christmas for the last five years," the bus driver grumbled. "You girls must be rich, going skiing and all."

"We saved most of the money ourselves," Cee Cee protested. "And we got a great package deal."

"Yeah," the bus driver agreed. "The old place has a hard time filling up, even during Christmas week."

"Why?" Lauren asked. "No snow?" She remembered that her folks never went to Mount Paradise until late in the season. Ever since Cee Cee brought the brochure with the special coupons to school last spring, Lauren had worried that the skiing might not be any good. There had been very little snow so far this winter.

"They've got snow machines now," the bus driver said in answer to her question. "But they just put them in and the resort's been pretty much off the map for years. Too much competition. Not enough excitement."

Cee Cee groaned. "I was afraid the deal we got was too good to be true."

The bus was climbing fast now, turning sharply as it maneuvered the steep curves. Jessica could see why the driver had been so reluctant to take them all the way. On the other hand, they'd bought tickets to Mount Paradise Lodge, not the village below.

They made one last, sharp turn and the lodge appeared in front of them. "Looks just like the brochure," Cee Cee said. She sounded happy and surprised. The lodge was a large, dark brown wooden building with three stories. There were many windows and each of them had an artificial candle in place for the holidays. The porch and roof were strung with red and green Christmas lights as well.

"We're here," the bus driver said. "Hop on down."

As they walked toward the lodge, Jessica whispered to Tonya, "You got us here. You were terrific."

"Assertiveness training, remember?"

"Yes, I remembered the words, but only after you said them," Jessica said. Tonya always seemed to know what to say. Once, Cee

Cee had suggested that Tonya was so competent because her father was a high-powered attorney. Jessica thought it was probably as much a result of dealing with being African-American in a school that had very few black students.

They stopped as they reached the front porch steps of the lodge and let their bags drop for a moment. Jessica asked softly, "What do you think?"

"I think it's old," Tonya answered tentatively. "And if our room hasn't had any more recent repairs than the lodge, I think we're in trouble."

Jessica nodded. Four girls in two beds would be a tight squeeze but it was the only way they could afford to take the trip and the picture of the room had made it look large. "Lauren said the food is good," Jessica said hopefully.

"Lauren was ten when she was here last," Tonya answered. "But skiing makes all food taste good so I'm not worried about that. How about we stow our gear and check out the coffee shop?"

"Not me," Cee Cee announced. "I'm going to the spa."

A tall young man with blond hair came out of the lodge and said, "I'm Marshall. May . . . may I . . . may I help you with your bags?"

He seemed very shy and kept looking at Lauren.

"Oh yes, thank you," Cee Cee said in a sweet voice.

"We can manage," Tonya answered at the same time.

Jessica leaned over to Cee Cee and said, "He works here. We'd have to tip him."

"I don't care," Cee Cee answered. "He's *darling*!"

By then, the young man was putting their bags onto his cart. He had a lot of trouble and bags kept slipping off. It was clear that he was new to the job. He also seemed to be hypnotized by Lauren who didn't seem to see him at all.

"Let me help," Tonya offered and expertly piled the bags for him. That seemed to make him more nervous and he looked around anxiously to see if anyone was looking. "Do you push it or pull it?" Tonya asked. "Want help?"

"Oh, no," he said, and began pushing the cart across the porch as the girls followed him. Tonya watched him lose two bags and pile them back on. He never took his eyes off Lauren during the whole process.

Tonya went to the front desk and registered for them all. They'd agreed in advance that they would use her dad's credit card and split the expenses when they checked out. "*Everyone* pays before you leave," her dad had warned them and Tonya knew he meant it. She'd have to watch Cee Cee. Cee Cee could get a little carried away when it came to money.

Tonya found their room and got there just as Cee Cee was giving the bellhop a five-dollar tip. She smiled her best smile as she said, "Thank you, Marshall. Will we see you in the lounge later?"

He quickly shook his head. "I work here."

"I know that," Cee Cee laughed, and tossed her head a bit as she looked up at him. "But you don't work here all the time, do you? What is there to do at night?"

"No." He was blushing a bright red now and looking down at his feet. Every few seconds he would look up at Lauren and blush an even brighter shade of red.

"So what do you do for excitement?" Cee Cee asked.

Marshall looked startled at that question and mumbled, "I study a lot," then dashed out of the room.

Jessica laughed but Cee Cee refused to have her dreams crushed. "I think he liked me," she said, "don't you?"

"I think your dire predictions came true,"

Tonya teased. "He couldn't see anyone but Lauren and she made him so nervous we're lucky he got our bags to the room. And five dollars for a tip! Cee Cee, you'll be out of money by Tuesday at this rate."

"I'm not eating a lot," Cee Cee announced. She rifled through her suitcase and pulled out two swimsuits. They were both very brief and very bright. She held them up and asked, "Shall I wear the pink and chartreuse or the yellow and blue one?"

"It doesn't matter," Lauren said. "You'll look wonderful in either one."

Cee Cee smiled at the compliment. "I'll be using them both a lot before the week is out. The picture in the brochure makes the spa look absolutely fabulous."

"So did the picture of our room," Tonya teased. The girls looked around at the small room. There were two windows which looked out on the forest, just as the photograph promised. Everything was exactly the way it appeared in the brochure, and yet the bedspreads were old and dingy and the room was much smaller than they'd imagined.

"I'll sleep by the window," Lauren said. "I don't mind the cold."

"We can stow our suitcases under the bed,

and use the dresser for our hair stuff and makeup," Jessica added.

"It'll be a great week," Tonya promised. "We'll be out so much that a small room won't matter that much."

"I wonder how they do it?" Cee Cee said softly. No one asked her what she meant. They were all wondering exactly the same thing. How could the brochure be so accurate and yet tell so little about the accommodations?

"Who wants to use the bathroom first?" Jessica asked.

"I do. I want to change," Cee Cee answered. "Anyone else going to the spa?" She didn't seem the least bit disappointed when they said no.

Tonya quickly and methodically hung her clothes in the closet. She had brought a parka, a dark blue and a bright red sweater, a white sweater and gray wool pants, Levi's, and three ski outfits, ski boots, and flats. She was ready to go.

Lauren watched Tonya unpack. "How did you ever get to be so efficient?"

"I was born that way. Come on, let's get you unpacked! She bent over to help Lauren take her things out of her suitcase. Funny, Lauren always looked so glamorous, but her clothes were a rumpled mess in the bottom of the suitcase. Tonya shook them out carefully and hung them on hangers. As she did so, she realized that Lauren had brought the fewest and the plainest clothes of any of them.

Cee Cee's clothes were always so bright that they attracted a lot of attention and she had lots of them. Tonya and Jessica dressed conservatively but they had brought their best winter sportswear and each had bought a new ski outfit to bring on the trip. They might not be flashy but they were certainly well dressed. But Lauren! Lauren had just stuffed some old clothes in the bottom of her suitcase and that was that. She was wearing some old Levi's and a gray-and-white Scandinavian sweater that was a little too short. The clothes in her suitcase were worse. One was a pair of khaki-green stretch pants. "Where did you get these?" Tonya asked gently.

Lauren smiled. "I found a lot of these in the attic when I started going to Maine with Brian. They were my mother's. I mean, my real mother's."

Tonya knew that meant they were at least seven years old.

"We used to come here a lot when I was a kid," Lauren said. "We skied somewhere nearly every weekend."

"How old were you when you started skiing?" Tonya said.

"Six," Lauren answered. "I learned right here on Shawnee Slope. That's the bunny slope. It's not Switzerland but it's nice."

Tonya nodded her head. "Yeah, skiing in Switzerland was different."

"Do you miss it?" Lauren asked.

"Nope. There's no place like home." Tonya tried not to be bitter as she remembered that after her father had worked abroad, her parents had moved back to the States so she could have a "normal" school life. Now she was being torn up in the middle of her junior year. Not exactly normal! She knew she couldn't really blame her father for taking the job in the new president's administration as an economic advisor but she didn't like the idea one bit.

"We moved a lot when I was in elementary school," Tonya said. "So I skied all over the Alps. But I really haven't done much since then. Just that weekend I went with you and Brian to Maine, and a couple of other times."

"Your father's very busy," Lauren said. She wished everyone would stop reminding her of Brian. It was bad enough that *she* thought about him all the time.

"I'm still pretty good, I hope." Tonya said.

"You're great about unpacking," Lauren

sounded so grateful that Tonya laughed.

By that time, Cee Cee was out of the bath-room and dressed in her chartreuse bathing suit. She looked around at her friends and asked, "Do I look terrific or what?"

"Terrific," they all assured her, although privately each thought Cee Cee's pert face and bright red hair would show off more in a plainer suit.

"Not a lot of room here," Cee Cee said. She opened the door and stepped out into the hall-way. Then she picked up her imaginary guitar and began her routine again.

She was so busy singing and dancing that she didn't even notice the three people who walked up and waited politely for her to stop dancing so they could pass. It was Lauren who stopped laughing long enough to point to the older couple and the young man with the bright red hair who were standing, smiling at Cee Cee.

Once Cee Cee saw them, she made a run for the room and dived onto the bed. The people passed and Cee Cee raised her head and asked, "How long was he out there?"

"Not long," Lauren assured her.

"Did you see him?" Cee Cee asked.

"Yes."

"Was he as *darling* as I think he was?"

"Yes," Tonya answered. "He was absolutely *darling*. He had exactly the same color hair you have and he had a nice smile. What more could you ask for?"

"Did he look like he thought I was a silly nut?"

"You *are* a silly nut," Tonya teased.

Cee Cee was pulling on her hot-pink ski pants and her black turtleneck sweater. "I'm going after him," she said.

"I thought you were going to the spa," Jessica said.

"Not if I can find the man of my dreams. That red hair must mean we're soul mates." By then, Cee Cee was out of the door.

Chapter 6

There were three television sets tucked around in corners of the lobby with several chairs in front of them. Tonya noticed that several families were watching holiday television specials. Poor Cee Cee, she thought. There's no one our age anywhere around. Just parents and kids or older couples.

The coffee shop was practically empty and there weren't any young people there, either. But the food was good, just as the brochure promised. Jessica ate a cheeseburger with fries and then had a piece of apple pie.

"Looks like you didn't have much Christmas dinner," Tonya commented. She and Lauren had split a tuna fish sandwich.

Jessica smiled and said nothing. She was glad she had come. It was good to be with friends. As she sat back in her chair and tried to relax, it seemed to her that she would never live through anything more difficult than the last three days.

Her mother had been semi-hysterical ever since the first X rays, and Jessica and her father had cooked the turkey dinner, wrapped the presents, and did everything they could to keep Christmas normal. They'd done well enough until Jessica said something about going on the ski trip and her mother had really fallen apart.

Her mother's eyes were wide as she said, "You can't possibly be thinking of going on a skiing trip now."

"No, I'm not thinking about it, Mother, I'm going," Jessica answered.

"You can't go on a ski trip when you're facing these test results," her mother had said.

"No matter what the results are, Mother, I can go skiing. Even if I'm diagnosed as having a brain tumor."

"*Don't* say that," her mother said. "That's impossible to even think of."

"Then if it's impossible to even think of, I might as well go skiing." Jessica had smiled and patted her mother on the arm. "Don't worry, Mother, I'll be fine."

"But *I* won't!" Her mother rushed from the room in tears.

Jessica sighed and said, "I really want to go,

Dad. It's important to my friends and I need to get out."

Her father patted her hand and said, "Go pack. I'll talk to your mother."

So in the end, she'd gone on the trip and she *would* be fine; Jessica forced herself to believe that. This will seem like a bad dream on Monday, she thought.

"Want to go into the lounge?" Tonya asked.

Jessica shivered.

"The lounge? Want to go?" Tonya repeated.

"Can we?" Jessica asked. She felt as though she was being awakened from a deep sleep.

"I'm not sure we should," Lauren said.

"Anyone can," Tonya answered. When Lauren looked as though she might argue, she continued, "You're the one who told us you used to sit in the bar with your folks, Lauren. It's a family lodge, remember?"

"I suppose we could have a Coke," Lauren agreed. Then she looked at her watch and said, "It's only eight o'clock but I'm sleepy."

I'll have to help her have fun, Jessica thought. Everyone knew Lauren depended too much on Brian and when Brian dropped her, she'd been like a little lost child.

Brian wasn't so special but Lauren thought he was. They'd spent so much time together that she really didn't have many friends except Cee Cee, Tonya, and Jessica.

This was a very difficult time for Lauren, Jessica knew, but she wished her friend would try a little harder. What would Lauren do if she were facing serious trouble the way she was? Jessica was surprised at the bitterness of her thought. "Come on, Lauren," Jessica said. "It will be fun."

Chapter 7

Cee Cee finally did go to the spa and was really pleased to see that the exercise rooms and spa looked exactly like the photograph in the brochure. The spa was a gigantic round circle, which probably could hold about twenty people, and the room was all dark wood with bright blue tiles on the floor. There were French doors and windows all along the wall that led to the birch forest and there was some soft music playing from hidden speakers.

Perfect, Cee Cee thought and she quickly got out of her pants and sweater and slipped into the hot water, trying to appear casual and relaxed as she looked around to see who else was there.

It took her a few minutes to realize that all but four of the twelve people were middle-aged couples. However, there were three really good-looking guys who were apparently alone. One of them was so good-looking that she was almost glad she hadn't been able to catch up with the red-haired man of her dreams.

Cee Cee smiled at the fellows and hoped that they would come over to her. As she smiled, she noticed that the three guys were all very blond and all very attractive.

One of them looked a lot like the guy on the cover of *Powder*. He had a square jaw and light blue eyes and looked like a movie star. The other two were just nice-looking guys. They seemed to be young, although she would guess they were in their early twenties. That was all right. Cee Cee had made the other girls promise they wouldn't tell anyone how old they were. She figured they would have a much better time if everyone thought they were in college, rather than high school.

The three fellows were talking in a very animated fashion with each other and didn't seem to notice her. Cee Cee tried closing her eyes and sinking up to her neck in the hot water so she would appear to be having a very good time without paying any attention to them.

She couldn't stand it with her eyes closed though, so she opened them and stared up at the ceiling at a fading mural of skiers wearing old-fashioned sweaters and face masks skiing around the room in a circle. It reminded her of an old mural in the town library and she decided it was painted at about the same time. That would have been sixty years ago. No wonder it was fading.

She raised her head and looked in the direction of the three fellows, saying, "Look up there on the ceiling. There's a really funny old mural."

One of the guys smiled and said, "Have a good evening," as they left the room.

There was no one in the hot tub except two middle-aged couples, who were only paying attention to themselves, and a really good-looking woman, probably in her thirties, who was with a silver-haired, distinguished-looking man about fifty. The woman, who had auburn hair, had her head on the man's shoulder, and he had his arm around her.

Cee Cee wondered if the man was a senator or something; he certainly looked very important. Everything about him had a distinguished, elegant air that you see in movie stars. She was idly letting her mind speculate about who and what the glamorous couple might be when a very beautiful teenaged girl with brown eyes and very creamy skin came up to the couple. The girl had thick, dark-brown hair that fell to her shoulders and moved gracefully when she turned her head. She sounded impatient as she said, "Daddy?"

The man turned his head up and said, "Hi, Angel. How are you? Are you having a good time?"

Angel frowned slightly and said, "Not really. I'm getting tired of being alone so much. I thought you and Madeline were going to have dinner with me this evening."

Her father sighed and said, "No, dear. We've been invited out with the Redmonds for dinner. You'll have to manage on your own."

The woman he was with said, "Oh, it's time to go. Come on, Stewart." They jumped up out of the tub and wrapped themselves in matching thick terry cloth robes. The girl was standing there, looking very uncomfortable and very alone.

Cee Cee moved over toward her and said, "Hi. Have you been here a long time?"

The girl frowned and turned away, then turned back and said, "I've been here about three days with my father and his new wife." Then she made a funny little face and said, "I guess a teenage daughter is just extra baggage on your honeymoon."

Cee Cee asked, "Coming in the hot tub?"

The girl shook her head and said, "No, I

52

think I'll go into the lounge." Then she stopped and smiled and asked, "Want to come with me?"

Cee Cee knew she should have her head examined for taking up with this beautiful girl. It was bad enough having Lauren along and now this one would be just so much more distraction. But she felt sorry for her so she said, "Sure. I'm turning into a prune anyway. I think my three friends might be there. Is your name really Angel?"

"Yes, what's yours?"

"Cee Cee. Really, it's Celeste Anne but no one calls me that. You'd better not try it, either."

Angel laughed and Cee Cee thought it really sounded like an angel's laugh — a sort of light, tinkling sound. "I wouldn't dare," Angel assured her.

"We're here for a week," Cee Cee confided. "How about you?"

"For an eternity," Angel said. "I can't believe I let my mother push me into making this trip with my father. It's his honeymoon and she only sent me along to be mean. They've been divorced for ten years but she's still mad. Even if he does still pay a lot of alimony and let her live in the Beverly Hills house."

"You live in Beverly Hills, California?" Cee

Cee had to admit she was impressed.

"During the school year," Angel said. "The worst of it is that my boyfriend lives there only in the summer. That's really why I'm here. Davey, that's my boyfriend, lives in New York in the winter and Beverly Hills in the summer. I live in California in the winter and Long Island in the summer. We hardly ever see each other, so when he got a job here, I came to visit."

Cee Cee wondered why Angel talked so much about personal things. Maybe that was the way people in California acted. And whose idea was it really that she was here — hers, her mother's, her boyfriend's, or her father and his new wife's? It was all pretty confusing but it was clear that Angel needed friends. "Come on to my room," Cee Cee said. "I'll just change clothes and we can hunt up the girls."

Angel came in and sat on the bed while Cee Cee dressed in her best kelly-green tights and purple and yellow sweater. The sleeves on the sweater were loose and flowing.

As Cee Cee fastened her orange and purple dangle earrings, Angel looked around curiously and asked, "You mean all four of you sleep in this one room?"

"Yes, we were lucky to get a package deal," Cee Cee answered, "the room, breakfast, and ski tickets for one glorious week." She looked at Angel's expensive clothing and gold jewelry and said, "I'll bet you have your own room."

Angel shrugged her shoulders and said, "My dad took the biggest suite. I have two rooms all to myself. So I sort of rattle around. My dad knows the manager here."

"What about your boyfriend?" Cee Cee asked.

"He works a lot," she answered very quickly.

"Well, you can tag along with us," Cee Cee offered. As Cee Cee put on makeup and combed her hair, she found out that Angel was seventeen and went to Beverly Hills High School which was better than any private school and that her boyfriend was eighteen and had just graduated from a private school in New York City. Cee Cee guessed he must be rich, too.

As Angel was relating all of this, she was looking at herself in the mirror, arranging her hair, putting on lipstick, and making herself as beautiful as she possibly could.

Cee Cee said, "I think it's wonderful that you know the manager of the ski lodge. Maybe you can get us some discounts for the dining room and coffee shop."

Angel shook her head. "No, I don't think so. I don't think my dad would want me to ask. Business is business, you know. But I can get us a good table in the lounge this evening. My boyfriend is entertaining."

"He's a musician?" Somehow, she had imagined he was a ski instructor although Angel hadn't said so.

"He sings and plays the piano and guitar. His name is David Rush."

"Did he come with you?" Cee Cee asked.

"No, he's been here all season. His mother got him this job because he wants to be an entertainer, but his father wants him to be a lawyer. And my mother's first ex-husband's brother married the sister of the fellow who owns the lodge and they owe him money so Davey got the job." When she saw the bewildered look on Cee Cee's face, Angel shrugged her shoulders and said, "Oh well, it's probably too complicated."

"Sounds very jet-setty," Cee Cee said. Then she asked, "Your Davey must know all the guys who work here? Right?"

Angel shrugged her shoulders again. "Maybe."

Cee Cee's eyes were round with pleasure as she said, "So, now that I know you, I know everyone. You're one of the rich and famous, and here I was, feeling sorry for you because you seemed so lonely."

A slight frown crossed Angel's face and Cee Cee thought she should try to be a little more careful about what she said in the future. Angel could be the key to a bright and shining social life. Cee Cee said, "Let's go."

As they walked down the hall Angel told her all about the place, saying, "You'll find that there's not a lot to do here. The bigger lodges have so much more. I've been to Aspen and Squaw Valley and lots of really great places. This is the pits."

"It's the biggest and best ski resort I've ever been to," Cee Cee admitted. "We decided last Easter to come here. We've been saving for ten months, so we're going to love it — no matter what."

When they walked into the lounge, Cee Cee saw that the girls already had a good table close to the small stage where a young man sat behind the piano, playing. She whispered to Angel, "Is that Davey?"

Angel nodded her head and Cee Cee introduced her to Tonya and Lauren. Angel's eyes opened wide when she met the girls, and Cee Cee couldn't tell whether the surprise was because Tonya was black or because Lauren was so good-looking.

Her reaction to Tonya wasn't important, Cee Cee thought. A lot of people were surprised to see the four of them always together — three white friends with one African-American friend.

Cee Cee thought to herself that Angel was probably used to being the prettiest girl in the room. Of course, when Lauren was in the room, that title went to her, hands down. Cee Cee guessed they wouldn't be seeing much of Angel after all. Too bad, Cee Cee could kind of sympathize with Angel.

Angel was small, with a beautiful classic face, but she was only about five feet four. And while she had a trim figure, it was not a figure that would stop traffic. Tonya and Jessica both had better ones, Cee Cee thought, and maybe she did, too, if the truth were told.

As she and Angel sat down, Cee Cee noticed that Angel wore quite a bit of makeup. She darkened her eyelashes with mascara and there was a faint hint of lavender eyeshadow on her eyes. She wore coral-pink lipstick, and the first thing she did when she sat down was pull out a compact and check that her cupid's bow mouth was perfectly drawn. This is a girl who likes to look in mirrors, Cee Cee thought. Funny how someone could come across as so self-confident yet need to constantly be reassured by her own appearance.

Chapter 8

"Guess what?" Cee Cee asked. "Angel's boy-friend plays here. Isn't that exciting?"

"He does the between-acts music," Angel said. "He's here for the whole season. He does the piano bar later."

"He's very good," Jessica said.

"Jessica is a musician, too," Cee Cee said. "She won a prize in junior high."

Angel smiled but Jessica had the distinct feeling that she wasn't impressed. Cee Cee was so unself-conscious that it was embarrassing sometimes.

Tonya added, "Jessica sings and plays the guitar."

"That's nice," Angel said.

Jessica thought perhaps that was enough on that subject.

The lounge was a medium-sized room with a bar in one corner and a stage with a piano at the other. There were tables and chairs that would hold about one hundred fifty people, but Jessica guessed there were only thirty or forty people watching the show.

When Angel's boyfriend, Davey, finished playing, he didn't join them. He simply bowed in their direction and walked off the stage. "He's not supposed to be too friendly," Angel explained.

They drank Cokes and watched a magician and then four showgirls did some dance routines. The lead act was a young man with very long hair, who used too-loud acoustics for his guitar. "Your friend is much better," Jessica said.

"I should hope so," Angel answered. "Davey's studied with some great Hollywood musicians. He's also an actor, you know. He's been in several movies."

Jessica was surprised by that information. Davey certainly didn't seem like the movie-star type. Until Angel arrived, she'd figured that he was a local college boy.

When it was Davey's turn again, he came out onstage, made a little half-bow, and smiled. Jessica thought he had a really nice smile. He wasn't handsome, but he had a *nice* face, and dark brown hair and eyes. When he smiled, there was an aura of happiness about him and he was obviously very comfortable onstage.

He said, "I'm the between-acts entertainment. They hired a kid like me because I know a lot of old-time songs. So, settle back and just relax." Davey began to strum on his guitar, starting out with "Hey Jude." Then he sang "Peggy Sue" and "La Bamba." He closed with a Michael Bolton song.

Jessica thought it was funny that all during the act Davey never once looked at their table. He had been smiling and gracious to the other people, but never acknowledged that Angel was sitting there with friends. She wondered about that, but when the act was over, Angel stood up and said, "Let's follow him into the piano bar."

"But I want to see the magician again," Cee Cee protested.

"You'll like Davey," Angel promised. She stood up, and all of the girls followed her. Jessica thought, She's used to getting her way. They all walked out of the lounge and across the hall to where several couples sat around a big stone fireplace and talked.

"This is more like it," Cee Cee said. "This looks like the picture in the brochure." One reason she had insisted on coming to Mount Paradise was the photograph of several young couples laughing and talking beside that big open fireplace.

Davey went to the other side of the room where there was a shiny black grand piano surrounded by a horseshoe-shaped bar. He sat down and began to play. No one looked up. There were people standing around with glasses in their hands, talking. A few were on bar stools but no one was paying any attention to Davey. Jessica felt kind of sorry for him.

Angel said, "We'll sit at the bar."

"I don't think we should," Jessica answered. "We don't drink."

"You don't have to drink," Angel said.

"But we're underage," Jessica protested.

"That doesn't matter as long as you don't drink."

"But is it fair for us to take up those seats?" Jessica asked.

Angel didn't even answer her. She just turned and pointed and said, "Sit here." Each of the girls sat on the bar stools around the piano. Angel smiled sweetly at Davey and said, "I brought my new friends to hear you tonight, Davey."

Davey nodded his head and said, "Hello, Angel."

"I want you to meet them all. This is Jennifer, no Jessica, that's correct, yes Jessica, I forgot," Angel said impatiently. "This is Jessica and Cee Cee and Tonya, and uh, what was your name, dear?"

Lauren blushed and said, "Lauren."

Davey nodded his head to all of them. Some other people sat down on the other side, and Davey turned immediately to the folks at the other end of the bar and said, "Anything special you'd like to hear?"

They all sat at the piano bar for about thirty minutes and Davey barely looked at them. Jessica thought Davey was behaving very strangely for a boyfriend and she wondered if they had quarreled earlier in the day. Jessica was getting uncomfortable and wondered if anyone else was. She looked over at her friends.

Cee Cee looked happy and Lauren was looking down at her Coke. No news there. Tonya looked as comfortable as she always did. One thing about Tonya, nothing ever seemed to ruffle her. No matter where she went, she always looked as if she were perfectly at home, and as though it were exactly the place she was supposed to be. Jessica had always admired Tonya's cool assurance and warm, friendly manner. In fact, Tonya was one of the people in the world that Jessica admired the most.

Sitting at the end of the bar, with her black hair and her soft brown skin and pale aqua sweater, she looked perfectly at ease, sipping her Coke. Jessica thought, She's the only black person in the room and it doesn't bother her. She has true self-assurance and it's based on knowing who she is. Jessica recognized and admired that quality in her friend.

Then she looked at Cee Cee and laughed. That Cee Cee! She had turned her back to Davey and was flirting with the three blond guys who were standing about twenty feet away. They were paying absolutely no attention to Cee Cee at all.

Cee Cee said, "Excuse me, I have to go to the bathroom." She got up and walked directly in the path of the three men, but they kept right on talking about snow conditions so she continued on to the rest room. On the way back, she stopped beside them and smiled sweetly and said, "Hi, my name is Cee Cee Davis. Didn't I see you three in the spa earlier?"

All three men looked at her. One nodded hello and then they went back to their heated discussion about how deep the powder was in the Rocky Mountains. Cee Cee tried to join in the conversation, "It doesn't really matter how deep the snow is there, you guys. We're here."

They acted as though she wasn't even there. Undaunted, she looked around the room for other prospects. There wasn't anyone else in the lounge under thirty. This was definitely a "family resort," as the brochure promised. They'd used that phrase in the brochure to persuade their parents to let them come to Mount Paradise, but Cee Cee had been sure that during the week between Christmas and New Year's the place would be full of college kids. Where were they?

A tall man with a reddish-gray beard came over and offered to buy Lauren a drink. "Oh no, I'm only sixteen," Lauren answered quickly. He went away and she scrunched down with her elbows on the counter and her hands half-covering her face. She had that half-smile on her face that meant that she was miserable.

Jessica glanced at her watch and bet herself that Lauren would soon be saying she was tired and would go to bed within fifteen minutes.

Jessica leaned over and touched Lauren's hand and said, "This is a sing-along. Let's sing along, shall we?"

Lauren shook her head quickly and said, "You know I can't sing."

"It doesn't matter," Jessica answered, and she opened her mouth and began to sing along on "Have Yourself a Merry Little Christmas" lending her good, strong voice to Davey's.

Davey looked up at her and smiled. Jessica smiled back, one musician to another. She knew that he had been having a hard time keeping the energy up and he would welcome help. When the song was over, he turned to her and asked, "Which one are you?"

"Jessica."

Davey smiled his wonderful smile and bowed his head. "I'm *very* glad to meet you. What's next, Jessica?"

Jessica asked, "Do you know 'Blowin' in the Wind'?"

"Sure, I was in the Boy Scouts," Davey answered and began to play.

About that time, two other couples came over, and they seemed delighted that there were old songs being sung. They joined in, and before eleven o'clock the bar was humming with guests, sitting around the piano bar singing their hearts out. Then Davey took a break and said, "I get fifteen minutes now, folks. I'll be back after my break." He got up from the piano bar and came over to Jessica and said, "You were great, Jessica. I hope you come back tomorrow night."

"I'd like to," she said. "I like to sing."

"Do you play?"

"The guitar and piano," Jessica said.

"Same as I do," Davey said with interest. "What's your specialty?"

"Just regular stuff," Jessica answered. "I've never done anything professionally."

At this point, Angel stepped in front of Jessica and said, "Didn't I tell you he was wonderful, Jennifer?" She stepped up on her tiptoes and kissed Davey on the cheek.

"Her name is Jessica," Davey corrected. Then he added, "Thanks for bringing your friends, Angel. They really helped." Turning back to Jessica, he said, "It makes a big difference when someone who can sing shows up. How long will you girls be here?"

"Till New Year's Day."

"Great! How about if I loan you my guitar tomorrow night? You can accompany me. Just strum a bit — nothing serious."

"Why not?" Jessica answered. She liked this young man and she was willing to help him. Besides, she had to get through Saturday and Sunday before she got her answer on Monday. It would take her mind off her troubles.

"*I'll* bring them all again tomorrow night,"

Angel promised, "and we'll have a good time. Oh, Davey dear, did I forget to tell you that my folks have gone to the Redmonds' this evening. They told me that you should be especially nice to me," and she slipped her arm through his and smiled at him with a possessive smile that was obviously meant to let Jessica know Davey was taken.

Jessica yawned as she said, "It was fun but I think I'll go to my room now." The last thing that she had on her mind was boys.

Lauren jumped up to join her and Davey called out to Jessica, "See you tomorrow night. Right?"

"Right," Jessica answered. It *had* been fun. Now if she could just get to sleep, this evening would be an unqualified success.

"Don't stay up too late," Lauren cautioned Tonya and Cee Cee. "We have a free lesson tomorrow morning. You wouldn't want to miss it."

"We won't be long," Tonya promised. "I'll see that Cinderella is home by midnight."

"Not if I find Prince Charming," Cee Cee warned.

Chapter 9

Saturday

The next morning the girls rose early and checked out the breakfast buffet. As the brochure claimed, there was a multitude of choices that ranged from cereals and pancakes to scrambled eggs and chicken livers. "Eat hearty," Tonya reminded them. "The best time to consume those calories is early in the morning."

"And the *cheapest*, too," Jessica added. Yet she could only manage some yogurt and a cup of tea. She'd slept well until five in the morning and then she'd lain awake, staring at the dark ceiling until the others rose at seven. Maybe she *should* have brought the sleeping pills Dr. Whitaker had offered her.

Cee Cee was as cheery at seven as she had been at midnight. "Look for that cute red-headed guy," she told the others. "He has to be around somewhere."

Marshall, the kid who'd brought their bags in yesterday, was their waiter this morning and he continued to stare at Lauren and blush. It would have been funny if Lauren hadn't been so embarrassed. Marshall would clear his throat and dart over to the table, asking, "May I bring you some more coffee, miss?"

When Lauren shook her head no, he'd blush and back off without even asking the others. Once, Tonya asked him for sugar and he brought it to Lauren. When Lauren went to the rest room, Tonya said, "If you ask me, those two are made for each other."

"They'd never get as far as last names," Cee Cee said. "I never saw two shyer people. Funny, I don't remember thinking Lauren was especially shy before this trip."

"It was because of Brian," Tonya observed. "She always had him to cling to."

Jessica laughed. "She's having growing pains, that's all."

"If she's having growing pains, she's really in trouble," Cee Cee said. "She's already taller than anyone on the basketball team."

"That's not true and it's not nice," Jessica said. "If I didn't know better, I'd say you're jealous."

"I *am* jealous," Cee Cee said cheerfully. "Come on, let's get moving."

It was a short walk from the lodge to the ski lift and they congratulated themselves for that. "At some resorts, you have to take a shuttle bus back and forth to get a cup of coffee," Cee Cee claimed. Since she was the one who'd found this place, she was clearly defending it.

"I like it here," Lauren said.

"So do I," both Jessica and Tonya assured her. Cee Cee seemed pleased by their loyalty. No one bothered to point out that she was the one who seemed most disappointed.

Cee Cee was wearing a new ski parka this morning and it was a medley of bright colors put together in a patchwork pattern.

Jessica had on her blue and purple ski jacket with purple pants. Tonya wore a navy-blue parka with red diagonals. Lauren's ski jacket was just plain black with a small bit of turquoise trim. Jessica's hat was blue, Tonya's was red, and Lauren's was black. Cee Cee didn't have a hat on even though it was bitter cold.

They were the first ones in the ski lift shack and Cee Cee and Jessica had their pick of boots to rent. Lauren had her own boots and Tonya had borrowed some from her cousin. Only Lauren had skis so the other girls took some time admiring the new equipment and selecting skis they were comfortable with. Cee Cee insisted on renting beginners' skis. The others tried to get her into something more advanced but she was determined, "I'm going to spend my time on important things, not skiing."

They were lined up at the ski lift before eight-thirty and while they waited, they tried to memorize all the ski lifts and slopes on their map. It was a cold, clear morning and they stood together, laughing and talking in anticipation of their free ski lesson.

"I'll bet our teacher is a gorgeous Norwegian." Cee Cee's eyes were gleaming with excitement and she was jumping up and down to keep warm. "Tall, blond, Nordic. Probably a sexy accent and of course, he'll prefer redheads."

"You should put your cap on," Lauren cautioned. "You lose ninety percent of your body heat through your head." Her black stocking cap completely covered her blonde hair. Even so, she looked elegant and rather mysterious.

"I'm not cold," Cee Cee said. But the tip of her nose was beet-red and there were tears in her eyes.

At exactly eight-thirty, the ski lift began to operate. The girls snuggled into the first two cars and they began the ride up the mountain.

"You know, Jessica," Cee Cee said, "that

musician was asking all about you after you went to bed."

"Davey?" Jessica was pleased that he'd asked about her. "What did Angel say to that?"

"She wasn't too happy," Cee Cee answered.

The ride didn't take long but it gave them a chance to see the layout of the resort area. They were going up Paradise Mountain and the lodge lay nestled in a small valley below. As they rode up, Jessica could see the birch forest that stretched along the road for several miles.

"Get ready," Cee Cee warned as the ski lift came in close to the top of the slope. Both girls jumped and tumbled into the snow. Jessica managed to get out of the way quickly but the lift attendant had to drag Cee Cee out of the line of Lauren and Tonya's hurtling bodies.

After they'd picked themselves up and dusted the snow off their clothes, Tonya turned and pointed and laughed. "Look there, Cee Cee, that's your Nordic ski instructor."

A tall, young black man was standing over on a knoll, waiting for them. He wore a bright blue jacket with the words MOUNT PARADISE written in large gold letters so he was clearly their instructor.

"I'm beginning to like this trip even more than I expected," Tonya said softly under her breath so that only Jessica could hear.

Jessica smiled at her friend. They both knew that one reason Tonya had so few dates at school was because she was black. The few white boys who had asked her out weren't that interesting and Tonya didn't know many African-American boys her age.

"How old do you think he is?" Tonya asked softly.

"Maybe twenty — maybe younger," Jessica answered. "He's young, that's for sure."

Tonya looked carefully at her new ski instructor. He did look young. He was six feet or more and slim. Somehow, Tonya knew he was very graceful even though he'd been standing absolutely still as they walked over toward him. He smiled broadly as they approached and said, "Welcome to Mount Paradise. You're here on a package tour, right?"

His voice was soft and warm. Tonya wondered why he had reminded her of pure motion even before he'd moved. Tonya was suddenly very shy and she was amazed by her reaction. She was never shy, but in the presence of this handsome young man, she felt as young and silly as Cee Cee or Lauren. She hoped no one would notice.

The wind was much sharper and colder on the top of the slope than it had been below.

Cee Cee was obviously freezing. She began to jump up and down vigorously, beating her arms on her chest and jogging in place. Their new ski instructor frowned and asked, "Don't you have a hat?"

"I'm not cold." Her teeth were chattering as she answered.

He shook his head with resignation and turned to look at the next group of four who were dropping off the lift. Obviously, he was accustomed to silly tourists.

Cee Cee, who was still jumping to keep warm, grabbed Tonya's arm and said, "Isn't he *darling*?"

"Quiet," Tonya frowned and then said in a whisper. "You think we have to like each other, just because we're both black? Is that right?"

Cee Cee blushed and stammered and said, "Well, you know, I just kind of . . . I just thought, um . . . If I offended you, I mean . . ."

Tonya laughed and shook her head. "That's all right. Maybe we *will* like each other, you can't tell. He is kind of cute." Tonya didn't look directly at him again until he called the group together and said, "I'm Jon Baker. I'm the head honcho — at least for the moment. Now we have to find out how well you can ski so we can see what to teach you. Okay? But first, let's go over a few things."

Two or three people grumbled under their breath. They obviously didn't want to stand still for long. Most of them were really bundled up in their turtlenecks and ski jackets. Any flesh that was exposed looked red and miserable. Cee Cee's face was as bright as her hair.

When Jon talked, he spoke softly but he had an intense look that made people listen. Tonya thought she could see a kind of crackling energy all around him but then she decided it was the reflection of the early morning sunlight against the snow. He was explaining that their free lesson included individual diagnosis and group instruction. "Then we'll recheck your form every other day while you're here," he said.

He went over some basic safety rules and then asked them to do some warm-up exercises, saying, "I know a lot of you have already done these but it's crucial for everyone to be ready. Let's start with some shoulder rolls."

They did about fifteen minutes of warm-ups and then he said, "Good. Now we're ready to ski. Ready?"

There were some groans and good-natured laughter and several people volunteered to be last. Jon smiled and led them up a little hill.

One by one, they had to ski to the bottom of the simple slope. Two or three people fell down, just on that little run. Jon sent them and a few other obvious beginners back up the little hill to work with an instructor who was waiting for them.

"Now I'll take you intermediates over there," Jon motioned his group to a different slope. "Let's begin by seeing how well you do on a real run," Jon said. "But before we ski, I'd like to go over the basics of skiing, just as a refresher, of course. The important thing is balance, and you have a natural center of balance in your own bodies. Along with balance, the next thing to be conscious of is flexibility. Skiing is a bit like dancing, in that your movements must be fluid and follow each other in a logical pattern. . . ."

Tonya was listening to the man, not the words. What sort of a person was he? He was quiet but he had authority. She thought to herself, This is a young man who will go far with whatever he chooses. She had to admit that she wanted to know him better. He was definitely the most interesting person that they had seen so far on this trip.

She let her thoughts drift. His words went on and she realized that the group was moving across the crusty surface of the snow toward the other side of the run. She followed without really understanding what they were doing or why.

They were standing at the crest now and Tonya could look out over the valley below. She breathed in the cold, clear snowy air and decided that she was very glad that she was here, very glad that she was going to be with her friends, and very glad that she was alive. As she looked over the valley, Jon continued talking.

Cee Cee poked her and said, "He's talking to you. He wants to know your name."

Tonya turned and smiled and said, "I'm sorry. My name is Tonya Jackson."

Jon nodded and asked, "Do you have any ski experience?"

"Yes, I'm a good skier," Tonya answered. "I skied in Switzerland."

Jon's eyebrows shot up and he said, "In the Alps?"

"Yes," Tonya answered, and she rattled off two or three resorts that she and her folks had gone to.

"Well, show us your stuff."

"Where do I ski to?" As she asked, Jon frowned, and she realized he had probably just gone through a whole set of instructions. "I'm sorry," she said.

"You go later." He turned from her and motioned to an older man who was standing beside Lauren. "You know where to go?"

The man nodded and shoved off, skiing down the short slope and turning in at the first flat spot. Jon nodded and shouted down at him, "Stay there."

"I can ski now," Tonya offered.

"Wait your turn." Jon's voice was almost impatient but not quite.

One by one, he separated the group into intermediate and advanced skiers. The intermediates went to the ski lift and took a ride up to the higher slope. The advanced group collected on a slope about five hundred feet below and waited for Jon.

Lauren was advanced, of course. Jessica protested that she wasn't very good but Jon said, "Every group needs a tail as well as a head. You can stay with your friends."

Soon, only Tonya and Cee Cee remained. Jon turned to Cee Cee and asked, "How about you? Are you an advanced skier?"

"No, I'm a beginner," Cee Cee answered. "Only I guess you call the beginners intermediates, don't you?"

"We do," Jon answered gravely. "Is that where you belong?"

Tonya looked at her in surprise and said,

"Cee Cee, you're a pretty good skier."

"I'm a beginner," Cee Cee insisted.

"You're as good as I am," Jessica pointed out.

Cee Cee poked her with a sharp elbow and repeated, "I'm a beginner."

They didn't argue. They figured that Cee Cee had picked someone out in the beginners' group that she wanted to be with. By this time, Cee Cee was making a great show of her awkwardness as she skied across to the other group. Tonya laughed aloud as she saw Cee Cee ski directly into the arms of her instructor.

Jon frowned at her laughter and said, "Okay, let's go."

As Tonya followed him down the hill, she decided that she didn't think he was so handsome after all. She was sorry she'd been caught not listening, but it wasn't exactly a crime. It was his job to be interesting, wasn't it?

Jon conducted the next two hours of the class as though she weren't even there. He only spoke to her when it was her turn to ski, and that was usually after he'd demonstrated a technique and given all of the others a chance to try it. Tonya wasn't used to being treated as the class dunce and she didn't like it one bit.

He was polite to everyone, she noticed, and never raised his voice or showed his impatience, even when a couple of the men who insisted they were intermediates turned out to be bad skiers. Jon Baker was quiet, serious, and so full of self-importance that Tonya wasn't sure she really even wanted to finish her free lesson.

Two women quit at ten o'clock, claiming they were too cold to continue. Jon nodded and let them go without comment. Then he turned back to the two older men and Tonya and Lauren and said, "You're all tougher, I guess. Lauren, let's go over your body movements again."

Lauren demonstrated the proper way to turn her body while skiing and Jon nodded in approval. "The important thing is to turn the body, shoulders first, not the hips. A good skier keeps that upper torso working. Now let's see you carve down the slope."

They watched as Lauren pushed off, moving in rhythmic turns down the hill. As she moved farther and farther away, she looked like a graceful blackbird with turquoise markings. She looked more at home than Tonya had ever seen her.

Jon said, "Your friend is good."

"So am I," Tonya snapped and immediately,

she was sorry. Now he would think she was as silly as Cee Cee.

Jon asked her, "How good are you?"

"I'm . . . I'm not as good as she is," Tonya stammered. She could kill him for making her so uncomfortable.

"But you skied in the Alps?"

"Yes, I have," Tonya answered. She didn't feel like telling him she'd been ten years old at the time. "But Lauren skis several times each winter."

"Couple of rich girls," Jon said softly, under his breath.

"I don't think you're supposed to make comments like that to the guests," Tonya said sharply.

"You going to turn me in?"

"I might," Tonya answered and she skied down the slope without saying any more.

But when she turned to look back up top where Jon stood he was laughing at her and he called down, "You *are* pretty good after all."

Tonya said to Lauren, "I'm going to quit now."

"No!" Lauren said with amazement. "I never thought you'd be a quitter — and on our first day."

"I'm just going to ditch the rest of this stupid lesson," Tonya said irritably. "I'll meet you for lunch and then we can ski some later. I hear that Indian Run is the best. Take the other ski lift."

Lauren shook her head in dismay but said nothing. Tonya turned and went toward the lodge without giving Jon Baker the satisfaction of looking back even once.

Chapter 10

At lunch Cee Cee entertained the others with stories about her adventures on the intermediate slopes. It seemed that her instructor was just adorable, and his name was Ian. She thought that he was the kindest, gentlest, sweetest man that she had ever met in her life.

As they ordered their food, Cee Cee jumped up and waved her hands and called out, "Ian, over here! Over here!" She was waving for him to join her.

He looked surprised but he did come over to the table, and asked, "Did you want something, miss?"

"Oh, join us for lunch."

The ski instructor said, "I would, but my wife and my son drove up from the village to have lunch with me, and I don't think there's room for three more people at this table."

Both Tonya and Jessica began to giggle. Just watching the look on Cee Cee's face was enough to make them glad they'd come on the trip. Cee Cee managed a weak little smile and said, "No. No, we thought you were alone."

As Cee Cee watched him walk away, she turned back to her friends and said, "He *was* darling but I really don't think it was fair for him to look so single. He wasn't wearing a wedding ring."

"He was wearing gloves," Jessica pointed out. "You can't see a ring under half an inch of wool."

"Maybe you should take up snorkeling," Tonya teased. It was the first thing she'd said all lunchtime.

Lauren asked Cee Cee, "*Now* will you join us on Indian Run?"

"What's so special about Indian Run?" Cee Cee asked.

"It's the best slope," Tonya answered. "The run is shorter than some of the others but it's more interesting with more turns, and besides, the lift lines aren't as long."

Cee Cee answered, "Lift lines are where you meet people. I guess I'll stay where I am. What about you, Jessica?"

"I promised I'd only ski in the mornings," Jessica reminded them. As she said the words, her sandwich turned to sawdust in her mouth. Couldn't she forget for even a little while?

"What are you going to do?" Cee Cee asked.

"I'm going back to my room and read. Maybe send some postcards."

Cee Cee looked disappointed. "I thought maybe you'd like to go into town with me."

"Town? Why? We just got here," Tonya asked.

"That's okay," Cee Cee said. "But I think I may come in early from skiing. We're never going to meet anyone if we always hang out together like this."

Tonya grinned and said, "Well, I already met the only unattached black man on the whole mountain, and Lauren nearly had that waiter trip over her this morning. Looked like Jessica was getting pretty friendly with that guy at the piano bar last night."

Cee Cee looked crushed. Then she said, "You're right. Every one of you has made more progress than I have. Life's not fair, is it?" Then she grinned and said, "But life is full of opportunities. Here come some right now."

Angel and the three fellows who were in the spa yesterday were heading toward their table. Linked in the arms of two of them, Angel was smiling broadly as she looked up at one and then the other, pretending to be surprised when she saw the girls.

When Angel and the boys were nearer, she called out, "Oh, come over. We're going to go sit at that big table, and I promised these guys that I had some darling girlfriends. Come on and join us."

Jessica shook her head. "I'm not finished with lunch yet."

Angel said, "But you are, Tonya, and you are, Cee Cee. Come on."

Cee Cee jumped up and said, "Sure, I'd love to." She ran over to Angel and the three boys as they selected a big round table. The other girls finished their lunch quietly, watching Cee Cee smiling broadly.

Lauren said, "Let's go back to the slopes."

"In a few minutes," Tonya answered her. "This is my first time on skis this year. I need to give my legs a little rest."

Even though Lauren had eaten as slowly as possible, she was finished. Jessica knew she didn't want to join Cee Cee and Angel so she asked her, "Do you want to go back to the room with me? I'm going to write some post-cards and read a book for a little while."

"I'd like that," Lauren said.

Tonya looked from Jessica to Lauren and said, "Cowards." Then she said, "Maybe I'll come with you." She stood up but she shook her head. "No, I think I'll give Angel and Cee Cee a hand and balance out the party. Tonya the good sport."

Tonya went to the other table where Cee Cee introduced her. "This is my friend Tonya. Tonya is the smartest and the cutest girl in our college, aren't you, Tonya?"

Tonya noticed that one of the young men had a strong French accent, and so she spoke to him in French. He responded immediately, in French, asking her how she had learned the language.

She said, in French, that she had learned it by living in France for four years. The two of them sat and talked about Europe for a while, while Angel and Cee Cee talked to the other two young men about ski conditions at the various resorts they'd been to.

Tonya could tell by looking at Cee Cee that she was having a good time. Why not? Tonya asked herself. They were attractive young men and they had good manners. Nothing like Jon Baker.

Tonya sat and talked to the young Frenchman much longer than she had intended to and from time to time, she found her eyes wandering around the coffee shop, wondering if Jon would come in for lunch. After an hour, she glanced at her watch and said, "This has been fun but I want to get some skiing in this afternoon, don't you, Cee Cee?"

Cee Cee looked at the two fellows and asked, "What do you guys want to do?"

The young Frenchman put his hand on Cee Cee's arm and said, "Unfortunately, Miss Cee Cee, we are leaving in thirty minutes."

It would have broken Tonya's heart to see the way Cee Cee's face fell if it weren't so funny. Poor Cee Cee — she'd just spent all this time flirting with guys who were going out the door!

"Have a good trip," Tonya said to cover Cee Cee's obvious disappointment. She took her friend's arm and dragged her out of the chair. "Come on, Cee Cee, let's go." And then Tonya stopped and said, "Angel, do you want to ski with us this afternoon?"

But Angel shook her head impatiently. She was looking toward the door, and Tonya caught a glimpse of Davey as he poked his head into the lunchroom. He was obviously looking for someone and it clearly wasn't Angel. He turned away without acknowledging them at all. Angel's face flickered with disappointment and then she tossed her head and smiled as though she hadn't even seen him.

As she and Cee Cee walked through the

door, Tonya said, "You know, I think Angel just invited us over there to keep those fellows with her so she could make Davey jealous."

Cee Cee shrugged and said, "Oh yeah, she's a real con artist."

"Then why do you want to spend time with her? Why fool with her? She's just using you."

Cee Cee just shrugged her shoulders and said, "I feel kind of sorry for her. And she knows a lot of people. She could be useful."

Tonya shook her head gently and said, "Don't you think that attitude makes *you* a little bit of a con artist, too? Cee Cee, you're not this boy crazy at home . . ."

Cee Cee reached out and put her hand on Tonya's arm. "Don't try to discourage me. This is a perfect opportunity for perfect romance. Mysterious strangers. Midnight rendezvous. Handsome young men."

"You're being silly."

"Don't dampen my spirits. This is my time to flower. I feel it here." She put her hand over her heart and said, "I just want something different to happen to me, I want a guy just for me. See you later. I'm going to check out the spa."

"I thought you were skiing?"

"I am, but I just want to duck into the exercise room and see if he's there."

"The redhead?"

"Yes. Or any other guy. We've only got six days left so I can't be too fussy." She laughed and ran out of the coffee shop.

Chapter 11

Later in the day, Lauren and Tonya took the ski lift to Indian Run, but Cee Cee decided to go on back to the Wayside where she'd skied with the beginners that morning. "Come with us," Lauren urged. "They say Indian Run is the longest and best slope."

"No." Cee Cee shook her head, "Even if Ian has a wife, if I stay on the easy slopes, I get to go up and down a lot more often and you meet new people each time. Besides the guy working the ski lift at the bottom is absolutely *darling*."

"Imagine that," Tonya said dryly. She was getting just a little bit tired of Cee Cee's nonsense. Besides, after her encounter with Jon this morning, she thought she might give up guys for good.

At Indian Run, when Lauren and Tonya got off the top of the ski lift and looked down, they were glad they'd decided to try it. "Gorgeous," Tonya said.

"Yes," Lauren answered. "I used to be too young to do this, so wish me luck." She bent her knees, gave a little push, and went down the long slope, turning and twisting to avoid the moguls and moving farther and farther away, looking very graceful and lovely as she descended to the open space behind the lodge below.

Tonya took a deep breath and pushed off, to follow her friend down the slope. For the first time all day, she felt really at home on skis and she loved the way that felt. Her face was tingling from the sun and she realized that it was a warm, beautiful day after all. Where had all the cold of the morning gone?

At the bottom, Lauren was waiting for her and she looked radiantly happy as she asked, "Try again?"

"Sure," Tonya answered. The two girls caught the ski lift and rode once more to the top. In all, they went down Indian Run six times and by four o'clock, they both decided it was getting cold and they were tired. "It's a lot for the first day," Tonya said. She was a little worried about Jessica being all alone.

"I guess we should quit," Lauren sighed.

"We can come back tomorrow," Tonya promised.

"Yes," Lauren agreed. Then she laughed and threw her hands up in the air, reaching high as though she could catch the sun which was still hanging above them. "Six glorious days of skiing. Isn't it wonderful?"

"Yes it is," Tonya agreed. It was good to see Lauren happy.

Suddenly, Lauren pointed toward a hill that had large outcroppings of rock on it. It was off-limits, of course, but there was someone coming down the slope.

Tonya saw Jon Baker racing down the unmarked trail, avoiding rocks by swift and expert turns as he moved so fast that she felt her heart beating in fear, just watching him. Suddenly, instead of swerving around a large outcropping of rock, he skied right over the edge into the air. As he fell toward the snow below, he turned a somersault.

"Look at your friend," Lauren said, awe in her voice.

Tonya didn't bother to object to the word "friend." She had never seen anyone actually do what Jon was doing except in ski movies. How did he do it? Those turns in the air like that? Where had he learned?

Jon landed easily, bending his knees and sliding along for a few seconds before he rose to jump once again as his skis flew through the air. This time, his jump was over a deep gorge and he twisted as he moved through the air to the other side. Tonya would never have dreamed of trying anything like that. Just the thought of going over such a deep drop made her heart stop. She saw him jump up once more, then kneel quickly and ski in a crouching position out of sight, behind the rocks.

Lauren said, "He's wonderful, isn't he?"

"Breathtaking," Tonya agreed. At least she knew one good thing about Jon Baker. He had spectacular talent.

"It must be wonderful to be that good at anything," Lauren said softly with awe in her voice.

"Yes," Tonya agreed. She could not get the image of Jon flashing through the sky out of her mind.

Chapter 12

Jessica walked down the long hallway to their room. She didn't really like spending a lot of time there — it was too crowded with everyone's possessions. Instead, she decided to get her book and find a nice, comfortable place to read.

She explored the old lodge, going up and down the halls and peeking into every door that was open until, finally, she found just what she'd hoped for. At the end of the second floor, there was a small room with a few books and chairs for reading. Best of all, there was a window seat that looked out onto the birch forest.

Jessica curled up in the window seat, warmed by the afternoon sun playing through the glass. She began one of the long books she'd brought with her on the trip. She was only on page five when she heard Davey's voice, "You'll get burned in that window seat. I know, I tried it the first week."

Jessica was surprised but not unhappy to see Davey. She marked her book with a finger and said hello. "I thought I'd found a secret room," she said.

"You have," Davey assured her. "No one ever comes here."

"You're here."

He smiled and slid into one of the carved chairs with the velvet upholstery and straight backs. "I come here every afternoon to practice. No one else has ever found this place. Not that anyone else was looking. Why aren't you out on the slopes?"

"Why aren't you?"

"I'm working," he reminded her.

"Don't you ski at all?"

"I'm not very good," Davey explained. "And I sleep pretty late so by the time I get a couple of hours of practice in, I don't have a lot of time. Besides, I like walking better. How about you?"

"I like to ski but not all day," Jessica answered quickly.

"I hope you'll come to the piano bar tonight."

"I promise," Jessica said. "Just to make sure I stay awake tonight, I'd better go take a nap now."

Davey said, "I'll practice in my room. Or better yet, you could practice with me here."

"No thanks," Jessica said and stood up before he could protest.

"Jessica, I was wondering if I could ask you to come practice with me all afternoon. I don't mean practice all afternoon — I mean, I was wondering all afternoon. I have an idea for a round that I'd like you to help me with."

When she didn't immediately say no, he went on, "I thought maybe you'd like to sing onstage, too. Do you think that you would do that?"

"I'll help at the piano bar, for sure." She sat back down. He was a nice person and she really didn't need a nap. She was getting to think of herself as an invalid but she wasn't. And if she did have a problem, naps wouldn't help.

"Thanks." Davey seemed happy to have her company.

Well, fine. There was nothing she would rather do than sing songs right now. If she couldn't ski, at least she could sing.

Jessica was pleased and surprised how quickly the time went. She and Davey sang for about an hour and they discovered that they both had a fondness for old songs. He had a very low, pleasant baritone voice and her contralto blended well. She didn't have as big a voice as he did, but that didn't seem to matter to him. "It's not the Metropolitan Opera," he said. "You'll do fine."

When she insisted she had to leave, he said, "You know, you're quite good."

She shook her head and said, "No, not good enough. I had my voice checked out when I was about fourteen. We went to two singing teachers, and they both agreed that I had a pleasant voice. The kind of voice that ends up singing in churches."

"You're probably more interested in something else, anyway, aren't you?" Davey asked.

"Yes, as a matter of fact, I'm interested in quite a few other things," Jessica answered. "I'm interested in mathematics and literature, and I think I might want to be a writer."

"A songwriter?"

"Could be," Jessica admitted. "Once in a while I work out some songs on my guitar."

"I'd like to hear some of them," Davey said.

"Maybe you will," Jessica answered. "But tell me about you. You have a good voice, and you're already singing professionally. How old are you?"

"I'm eighteen," Davey answered. "I finished high school last June and took a six-month trip to Europe with my mother. Now I'm waiting to get into college next fall. So I took this job up here for the winter season."

He had a very direct and simple way of speaking. No attempt to impress her and yet, Jessica could guess that he was a very, very rich boy.

Perhaps he'd read her mind because he said, "I'm one of those people who isn't quite sure *what* to do with the rest of his life. Money isn't a major consideration."

"You mean you're loaded," Jessica teased him.

He smiled and said, "I guess that's what you could call it. At any rate, I could get by without working for the rest of my life, but I *want* to work. The problem is, I can't decide if I want to work as a stockbroker or as a musician."

"That's a funny choice," Jessica said. "When you sing, you seem as though you love it so much. It seems like it would be an easy decision for you."

"Music?" Davey sighed. "I suppose the typical plan would be to pursue a musical career — defy the stodgy family and all that. But my family is only half-stodgy. I'm in a position where I can't win."

"Or maybe you can't lose."

"Yes." He smiled quickly. Jessica noticed that he had a funny way of tilting his head slightly to one side when he talked about his family. Until now, she'd seen only a very straightforward, self-assured young man. Now she could see that he was still a boy — a boy who was anxious to please.

Davey seemed to want to talk about it. "The problem is, my mother is a failed singer. Well, I don't know if she really failed. I think what she really did was marry and give up her musical career. And so ever since I've been a little kid, she's been pushing me toward music. She actually managed to get me in a couple of movies when I was a kid. And I was on a TV series for a year until my dad put his foot down and sued for custody. He won."

"So now you live with your dad?"

"I go back and forth."

"Where is your father?" Jessica asked.

"He's in New York City. He expects me to go to Harvard and follow in his footsteps. My mother expects me to go to UCLA or USC while I break into show business. She got me this job."

"Yes, Angel told me," Jessica answered.

"What else did Angel say?" he asked.

"Not much." She stood up again.

Davey looked upset. "Angel and I have dated some, but it's nothing serious. Not to me, anyway."

"Is it to Angel?" Jessica asked.

Davey shrugged. "I don't know. Angel is . . . Angel."

"I really have to go now," Jessica said. "The girls will be waiting for me."

"But you will be there tonight?" Davey asked.

Jessica laughed. "You've asked me that three times now. I always do what I say, Davey. Don't worry."

Davey smiled and Jessica felt like patting his cheek or giving him a hug. She didn't, though. She was in no position to be nice to a little lost stray, who might be another girl's boyfriend.

Chapter 13

When they couldn't find Jessica, Tonya and Lauren went into the coffee shop and ordered hot chocolate. As they sipped their sweet drinks, Cee Cee came in and slumped down in the chair next to them, announcing, "I'm in love."

"Does he have a name?" Tonya asked.

"Everyone has a name," Cee Cee answered haughtily.

"But she doesn't know his," Tonya said to Lauren.

"Names aren't important," Cee Cee said. "Eyes are important. Eyes are the windows of the soul and when I looked into his eyes, I saw my soul mate. We were *meant* for each other."

"Then you'd better ask him what his name is, so you can tell him," Tonya teased.

"He's *darling*," Cee Cee went on. "He's got

dark brown hair and blue eyes and he's about six feet tall. Strong face."

Tonya half-listened to Cee Cee and thought about Jon. Why had they started off so completely wrong? This morning had been both their faults, really. He was quick to judge and she'd been at her worst. But no matter what else Jon Baker turned out to be, he sure could ski. How did he do those midair twists?

She wondered how old he was. He had to be at least eighteen to be working here. She sighed and drank her chocolate, burning her lip with the hotness of it. Why had she acted like such a brat? She could have at least found out where he was from and where he learned to ski.

He was definitely young for such an important job. He didn't seem to have much sense of humor. But then, she hadn't been very funny. I'll apologize, she thought. Next time I see him, I'll just tell him the truth — that I was nervous because I thought he was attractive and I'll tell him I'm sorry I acted like a brat.

"You aren't listening," Cee Cee accused.

"Maybe his name is Sam," Tonya answered. But her friend was right. She wasn't listening.

"Never mind," Cee Cee said. "I'll know by this time tomorrow."

When Lauren and Tonya laughed, Cee Cee continued her banter, "It's fine for you to laugh but I've got to work fast. I saw Lauren at lunch today and she had a long line of guys behind her."

"You're always teasing me," Lauren said. "No one has even talked to me on this whole trip."

"Oh no, they don't *talk* to you. They just *look* at you. They're afraid to talk to you. They just follow you everywhere. Don't you see them behind you?"

Lauren turned around and looked over her shoulder and said in a bewildered voice, "I don't see anyone."

"Well, they're there. You just don't notice them," Cee Cee said. "Want to go into town for dinner?"

"No," Tonya answered. "Joe's Diner doesn't look too appealing."

Lauren said, "You know, I think I'll go look for Jessica."

The minute she was out of hearing distance, Tonya said, "I want to talk to you seriously, Cee Cee. You've got to stop picking on Lauren."

"I was only *kidding*."

"It's not funny," Tonya said. "You've got the poor girl scared half to death."

"How could anyone who looks that good be scared?" Cee Cee asked.

"She's shy," Tonya answered. "And she misses Brian."

Cee Cee laughed. "Well, she can get all the replacements she wants if she'll just open up her eyes and look at what she's got going for her."

Tonya interrupted Cee Cee and said, "Cee Cee, stop teasing Lauren just because you're jealous of the way she looks. You look fine yourself."

Cee Cee turned bright red and stood up and put her fists on her hips and said, "Tonya, you talk to me just like my mother. I know what I'm doing. I'm just keeping everything light and cheerful. I'm *not* picking on Lauren."

"You *are* being rough on Lauren, and that's *not* being a very good friend."

Cee Cee was mad now. "You don't need to boss me around just because I want to meet some boys and have some fun. And I don't need to be told how to treat Lauren." With that, she turned on her heel and stomped out of the coffee shop.

"Where are you going?" Tonya asked.

"I'm going to exercise and then I'm going night skiing. Alone! Just get off my back!"

"What about dinner?"

Cee Cee was almost out of the coffee shop and she pretended she hadn't heard. Tonya sighed and drank her chocolate slowly, wondering if Cee Cee was right and she was too bossy. But it was natural to want to take care of your friends, wasn't it?

Tonya was afraid she was going to have to eat supper alone. Cee Cee was obviously mad and Lauren was hiding in her room, probably crying over Brian. When Jessica came into the coffee shop, Tonya looked up gratefully and said, "At least I have one friend left."

They ordered a light supper and Tonya told Jessica all about the quarrel she'd had with Cee Cee. Jessica listened thoughtfully until she was through and then she was silent. "You think I was too tough on Cee Cee?" Tonya asked. She expected Jessica to have some good advice, or think of a way to smooth things over.

But Jessica shook her head and said, "It's not your fault." Then she added, "I don't know what to do about Cee Cee. This trip hasn't gotten off on a good start, has it?"

Tonya nodded her head in agreement. "It's going to be a long week, what with Cee Cee acting like an idiot and Lauren acting like a heroine in a soap opera."

Jessica sat silent. She was thinking about her own personal drama that no one knew anything about. It made everything else seem so trivial. It was almost funny to think about things that you knew people would get over or outgrow, when you weren't sure you would live long enough to outgrow anything.

"Speaking of soap operas," Tonya said, "You look kind of down. You aren't really sick, are you?"

"No," Jessica said too quickly. "I'm just a little tired from the flu and I did promise my parents. Besides, all day on the slopes would be too much for me."

"It was a lot for me," Tonya said and she rubbed her thighs. "I really ache. Maybe I'll try out that spa that Cee Cee raves about. Want to come with me?"

"Sure," Jessica said. On the way to their room, Jessica told Tonya a little bit about her meeting with Davey. "He's a nice guy and I said yes without really thinking about it. So I guess I'm stuck."

Once they were in the spa, Tonya said, "I was rude to our ski instructor. I feel bad about it."

"Too bad. I thought you might like him," Jessica said.

"I thought I might, too, but we got into this silly argument."

"When you see him again, apologize," Jessica suggested.

"*If* I see him again."

"Checkup lesson on Monday," Jessica reminded her. "All is not lost."

Tonya felt better, just remembering that. "Maybe we should try and help Cee Cee find a boyfriend," Tonya said. "If she found someone she liked, she'd be off our hands."

"That would just leave Lauren," Jessica said. Then she laughed and suggested, "Maybe we can find someone for her, too."

"Twins," Tonya was really laughing now. "Or brothers or best friends so they had to double-date."

"Sounds like the perfect solution," Jessica said. "We'll start looking right away."

"I'll look on the slopes," Tonya was still laughing. Maybe she would look — and forget about Jon.

Chapter 14

Night skiing was cold, Cee Cee decided just a few minutes after she zoomed down the beginners' slope for the first time. And there weren't any interesting people out at night, either — just a bunch of young kids and old folks. Even the attendant on the ski lift was old. He had bags under his eyes and a graying beard.

Cee Cee jumped onto the ski lift. This time it was a three-seat lift, and a woman with two children pushed onto the lift with her. Cee Cee scooted over as far as she could and asked herself why she was doing this. Then she answered herself. I'll be darned if I'm going in and let Tonya tell me what to do. I'm tired of her telling me things. Tonya isn't in charge of the world.

The woman next to her said, "You should have worn a cap. You lose . . ."

". . . ninety percent of your body heat from your head," Cee Cee finished for her.

"I'm surprised your parents let you out dressed like that."

"I'm not here with my parents," Cee Cee said.

"Shame on them letting a young girl like you out alone in a place like this," the woman clucked and put her arms around her two children.

A place like this, Cee Cee repeated to herself. This is not exactly a place like this, lady. This is a place where your little darlings are perfectly safe and so am I.

Cee Cee couldn't tell under all those wrappings whether they were boy or girl children. All she knew for certain was that they were dressed warmly. She almost wished she were wrapped up as well. There were times when survival was more important than sex appeal.

As they reached the top of the hill, the woman pushed her two children off first, leaving Cee Cee on the lift as it started up again. When she jumped, she landed hard on the icy snow.

Cee Cee stood up and looked down the slope at the lodge below. The lights along the ski slope were red and green and they seemed to lead directly to the lodge. There were bright lights strung all over the lodge and it looked warm and inviting. She shivered and asked a man standing beside her, "How cold do you think it is?"

"Below freezing," he answered and then he frowned. "You should have worn a cap."

"Thanks for the advice." Cee Cee smiled sweetly and pushed off the slope. She might as well go back to the lodge and join her friends. Everywhere she went, people gave free advice. And at least the lodge was warm. Besides, they were all going to the lounge later in the evening and she wanted to go along. She was *bound* to meet someone interesting tonight.

When Cee Cee got back to the lodge, the others weren't there. She dressed quickly and went to the lounge where Jessica, Lauren, and Tonya were laughing at a baggy pants clown. She slid in beside them and grumbled, "This really *is* a family lodge. They even have kids acts at night."

"He was funny," Lauren answered, "and quite sophisticated, too."

Good, Cee Cee thought, at least she's speaking to me.

"How was the night skiing?" Tonya asked.

Cee Cee breathed a sigh of relief to find that

they were all friends again. "Cold," she admitted. "If I do it again — and I'm not sure I will — I'll wear a cap."

Tonya nodded. She recognized that Cee Cee was apologizing. Good, now maybe they could all have a good time. She looked around the room, hoping that Jon was there. No such luck.

Davey came over to their table and asked, "You guys coming to the piano bar?"

"Sure," Tonya answered and stood up. They all walked from the lounge to the piano bar with Davey. When they entered the bar, Angel was sitting on a stool with her stepmother and father.

Davey smiled and said hi and then slid into a medley of fifties' songs. Jessica joined him until she saw the storm clouds on Angel's face. She let her voice trail off and she said, "I wish everyone would sing."

"I like it better when just Davey sings," Angel said. "*He* has a great voice."

"Angel," Davey began, but Jessica held up her hand to stop him.

"I'm really tired," she said, "so I'll catch your act another time."

"I'm tired, too," Lauren said and slid off the stool next to Jessica's.

"Me too," Tonya said as she headed for the door.

Cee Cee only hesitated a moment before she joined her friends. The evening was over but tomorrow was another day.

Chapter 15

Sunday

Sunday morning they were out on the slopes by nine A.M.

The slopes were crowded with people who had come up for the day. That made the lift-lines longer than they'd been on Saturday, but the morning was still fun. For one thing, the weather was good with a strong sun and no cold wind. "Enjoy it," the guy at the ski lift told them. "Blizzard coming tomorrow."

"I hope not," Cee Cee wailed. A blizzard would spoil all their fun. Of course, sitting inside by the fire might be nice. "On second thought maybe blizzards are romantic," she said to no one in particular. Her friends were skiing the difficult slopes. She was sticking to her original game plan of staying with the beginners.

Jessica skied all morning and had lunch with the others. Then she decided to take a walk in the woods. The sun was shining and it was a clear day and she might not get another chance to really explore the woods. She bundled up and started out the door of the lobby.

Davey caught up with her before she was a hundred feet from the lodge. He called out, "Jessica, wait for me."

She waited although she really wanted to walk alone. The sun was so bright that she couldn't see Davey very well, even when he was quite close, but she could see Angel standing on the lodge porch, looking out at them.

"I'm walking into the village," Davey said. "Come with me?"

"Too far."

"It's an easy walk down and we can catch a taxi back," Davey urged. "I do it all the time."

Jessica hesitated. It would be fun to walk into the village but there was a problem called Angel, standing on the porch. "Is Angel coming?" Jessica asked.

Davey shook his head quickly. "She's having lunch with her parents and some of their friends. Command performance. But don't worry, I'm harmless."

Jessica laughed aloud.

"What's funny?" Davey asked.

"The idea that you *wouldn't* be harmless," she said.

"I'm not sure that's a compliment," he answered slowly. He seemed to be genuinely puzzled at her reaction.

She thought about explaining to him how nice and innocent he seemed but she supposed that might make it even worse so she just asked, "What's in town?"

"Not much," he admitted. "But there's a pretty good record store and they ordered some new sheet music for me last week. I thought we might pick it up. Mostly, it's just the walk."

Should she go on her own into the woods? If she did, she would just worry. Better to go with Davey. "Okay," she agreed, "but only if you promise we can actually get a taxi back."

"We can."

"When we arrived, there were no taxis."

"That's because Bert went to visit his sister for Christmas dinner. There's only one taxi in the village and it doesn't run on Tuesdays."

"It wasn't Tuesday when we came," Jessica said suspiciously.

"But it was Christmas Day," Davey persisted. "And this is just a simple Sunday. Everything is open on Sunday in Paradise Village. It's their biggest day of the week."

"You seem to know a lot about the village."

"I've been here two months, remember?"

Davey pointed to the top of one of the beeches and said, "Look, you see that tree? When I came it had long palm leaves."

Jessica laughed. "There are no palm trees in Vermont."

"There *were* two months ago."

They were walking pretty fast, partly to keep from getting cold, and partly because the road was so steep that it made walking seem a lot like running. At one point, Jessica slid a bit on the ice and Davey reached out to catch her. Jessica neatly avoided his grasp and righted herself.

"I said I was harmless," Davey said.

"So you did," Jessica answered. And then, because she thought her retort might have sounded as if she was flirting, she changed the subject. "Sing something for me."

"You're pretty good at handling people, aren't you? Did you learn to negotiate from your lawyer father?"

"Just sing," Jessica answered with a laugh. Actually, she'd learned most of what she knew about avoiding trouble from handling her mother but that wasn't anything she wanted to share with Davey.

"Are you like your father, Jessica?"

"Not really," she answered. "Are you like yours?"

"I'm not much like either of my parents," he admitted. "I just wondered if you were. It's something, isn't it — being an only child."

"I had a brother who died before I was born," Jessica confided. "My mother . . . my mother never really got over it. She worries too much."

"Is that why you can't ski all day long like your friends?"

"Partly," Jessica answered. "At the risk of having you say I'm trying to change the subject, I'd really like to hear about your life as a child actor. Was it as strange as it seems it would be?"

"Pretty strange," Davey agreed. "Imagine being a little kid who can barely read having to learn a lot of lines and do what they tell you all day long."

"So you hated it?"

"I didn't like it," Davey admitted. "It would have been different if we needed the money, of course."

"How would that be different?"

"Then there would have been a purpose to it all. As it was, I just did it till my dad rescued me."

"Do you think that's why you aren't sure about the singing? Because you hated the acting?" Jessica was beginning to see that beneath that simple, pleasant exterior, Davey was a pretty complicated kid with some very special experiences — and probably a lot of them were bad. Still, he seemed to be a happy enough guy. Happier than she was — at least this week.

"What are you thinking?" Davey's voice was suddenly soft, and concerned.

"Why?" Jessica asked.

Davey said reflectively, "You look all light and easy and then this shadow moves across your face and I think I don't know you at all."

"How could you know me?" Jessica said lightly. "We only met two days ago."

Before he could continue his line of questioning, she pointed ahead and said, "Look, there's Paradise Village. And I'm warning you right now, if we don't get a taxi, I'm hitchhiking back to the lodge."

"Don't worry," Davey assured her. "Bert will be there."

They spent a couple of hours walking around town looking at all the things that tourists might buy. Jessica selected postcards and wrote notes to her grandmother and Aunt Lee and mailed them. Then Davey took her to the record store and they looked through all the old sheet music. "Now I'll show you the movie house," Davey said. "In fact, if you want, I'll take you to the movies on Tuesday evening. It's my night off."

Jessica didn't reply. He hadn't mentioned Angel at all that day and she was glad for that. On the other hand, it was uncomfortable to have someone else's boyfriend talk about taking you to the movies. Did that mean he wanted her to come along with him and Angel? She wasn't quite able to imagine Angel allowing that.

By the time they got through with their shopping and sight-seeing, it was almost dark and Jessica was beginning to worry about the taxi that Davey had promised. "We'd better go," Jessica said. "Where's the taxicab?"

"We have to call from the diner," Davey answered. He took her hand and began to lead her down the street toward the diner. She let him hold her hand just long enough not to make an issue of it and then she pulled it away.

As they neared the diner, Davey said in a soft, worried voice, "Angel's here."

"I hope she's not mad at you," Jessica said.

Davey didn't even bother to answer her. He simply pushed open the diner door and strode in.

Chapter 16

At four o'clock Angel had knocked on the girls' door and asked if anyone wanted to go down into the village. Only Tonya and Lauren were in the room but Tonya said yes immediately and urged Lauren, "You come, too."

"I'm tired from skiing," she answered.

"Be a good sport," Tonya pleaded. She figured the drive into town would be good for them and it would keep Cee Cee and Lauren out of each other's hair for a while.

So Lauren and Tonya soon found themselves in Angel's bright red Camaro. As she sat down and snuggled into the leather upholstered seat, Tonya asked, "Is this yours?"

"Madeline's," Angel said briefly. "It's rented, of course." Then she added, "Madeline is my new stepmother."

"Why isn't she driving it?" Tonya asked.

"She's out with my dad in the Lincoln."

"Let me get this straight," Tonya said incredulously. "Your folks rented *two* cars for this trip?"

Angel shrugged. "Madeline is an independent woman."

"I guess so," Tonya said appreciatively. "What does she do for a living?"

"You mean besides marrying my dad? She's a lawyer."

"So is my dad," Tonya offered. Her father was very successful but there was no way that her family would even consider spending that kind of money. Angel must *really* be rich. Poor little rich girl, Tonya thought. Even if she was a spoiled brat, Angel probably had plenty of real problems. She obviously didn't get along well with her new stepmother and though she claimed Davey was her boyfriend, Tonya hadn't seen any signs of that.

Angel took the curves a bit faster than Tonya liked. At one point, Lauren suggested that she slow down so they could see the scenery. If anything, Angel went faster so Lauren didn't make any more suggestions.

The village was only at the bottom of the hill and it probably took no more than ten minutes to get there, but Tonya was very glad to be on solid ground again.

As Lauren unfolded from the backseat,

Tonya said, "You can sit in front on the way back."

"No thanks," Lauren dismissed her suggestion and her tone seemed to say she was as glad to be out of the car as Tonya was.

Angel looked up and down the street quickly and said, "There's a diner and a drugstore and some shops. Let's look in the shops first." She led them quickly down the street to a record store and stopped in front of the window, looking inside. The store had a few instruments in the window and a display of sheet music, too.

So that's what we're doing here, Tonya thought. We're looking for Davey. She almost felt sorry for the girl when it was clear the store was empty. But Angel didn't seem too disappointed. She led them on a short tour of the other dozen shops in the village, looking into each as she pointed out their limited offerings.

Then Angel said, "We might as well go home."

Tonya objected. "As long as we're down here, let's check out the diner. At least it will be cheaper than up at the lodge."

"Good idea," Lauren said and started into the diner.

Angel didn't look too happy but she came along quietly. As they walked in, everyone in the diner turned and stared at them. Tonya could see that this was really a local hangout. There were a group of older men who were drinking beer.

In the back of the diner, there were four teenage boys in Levi's and plaid jackets who were laughing and talking. When the girls walked in, the boys all stopped and stared at them.

Tonya supposed they didn't see girls who looked like Angel and Lauren and her very often. Angel was quite beautiful but, of course, they were all really staring at Lauren.

"Let's go," Angel said crossly.

"I'd like some pie and coffee," Tonya answered.

Lauren slipped into the booth with the fewest holes in the plastic upholstery and picked up a menu. When Tonya sat down opposite Lauren, Angel looked annoyed, but slid in anyway.

They ordered pie and coffee and as soon as the waitress left, one of the boys from the back came up and said, "I'm Jimmy. Are you girls from up at the lodge?"

"Yes, we are," Tonya answered. "Do you live here in town?"

"Oh, yeah, uh-huh, we do," Jimmy said. "We sort of hang out here to see who'll come down off the hill. Man shortage up there."

Lauren blushed and Angel frowned. Tonya laughed and said, "You might be right. But we're just seeing the sights."

"Oh, yeah," Jimmy answered. "That's what they all say. You girls looking for some entertainment?"

"No," Lauren answered quickly. "No. We're just on our way out of here."

A nicer-looking young man in a dark-green plaid jacket and short, dark curly hair stepped up and said, "Hi. Don't let Jimmy scare you. He's a little backward but harmless."

Tonya smiled and said, "We know that. We're fine." Then she added, "I'm Tonya and this is Lauren and Angel."

The young man said, "My name's Greg. And this is Jimmy."

Tonya asked, "Join us?" She could see how awkward and embarrassed they were . . . and young. She just wanted not to seem snobbish.

The young men looked surprised and pleased and Greg slid in beside Lauren, smiling at her. She quickly looked down at her apple pie.

"Do you go to school here in town?" Tonya asked.

"Oh, yeah, uh-huh, we do," Jimmy said. "Only we're on vacation now."

There was an awkward lull in the conversation until Greg asked, "Where do you girls come from?"

Tonya answered since neither Angel nor Lauren seemed to be willing to help keep things rolling. "Lauren and I are from Connecticut. Angel is from California."

"Oh." Jimmy didn't seem to be able to think of anything else to say.

There was more silence and then Greg asked, "Do you like to ski?"

"Yes," Tonya answered quickly. "I'm a pretty good skier. My friend is much better." She pointed to Lauren. Then it occurred to her that she'd never seen Angel on skis.

"We're pretty good, too. But only when there's real snow on the ground. We ski on our own hills. Can't afford the lodge's rates."

"Are there other slopes?" Tonya asked.

"Lots of places to ski. The only difference is you have to climb up the hill yourself," Greg said. "It's easier than you might think, though, because my dad drives one of the Sno-Cats, and we keep it in our yard. Sometimes I drive the Sno-Cat up to the top of the hill and ski down to the bottom. Then a friend drives down and picks me up and we take turns that way." He grinned again. "Takes a lot of gasoline, but it's cheaper than sixty-dollar-a-day ski tick-ets."

"We have a package deal for the week," Tonya said. "I would think they'd have cheaper rates for townspeople."

"They really don't want town kids up at the lodge that much. You know, a lot of our fathers work there, and basically we're supposed to stay away. You know how it is."

Tonya nodded. She didn't really know how it was but she could guess.

She fished around for another topic and wished someone else would help her. Greg was doing his best but she was beginning to feel as if she had been trapped at one of those awful cocktail parties her folks gave, where she was supposed to put in an appearance and smile until it was polite to disappear. Washington would be full of those — she didn't enjoy playing that game on vacation.

Still, she noticed that Greg kept looking at Lauren, although he was talking to her, so maybe it was worth the effort. He answered Tonya's questions, then looked at Lauren. All the time Lauren sat as cold and immobile as a snow princess, not saying one word.

Angel said, "We've finished our pie. Let's go."

"All right," Tonya agreed.

Greg said directly to Lauren, "But I don't know your name."

Instead of mumbling and ducking the way Tonya expected, Lauren answered, "Lauren Anderson."

He stuck his hand out to her. "I'm Greg McArthur." They shook hands gravely and he began to slide out of the booth.

"Let's have a refill," Angel said suddenly. She smiled at Greg and said, "You don't have to run away, do you?"

Tonya wondered what had cheered her up so quickly. Greg looked confused but happy to have a reprieve as he slid in closer to Lauren again. Lauren didn't look at him but he watched her every move.

"Hi," Jessica called out and suddenly Tonya understood everything.

Jessica and Davey were coming toward their booth. Once again, they were involved in Angel and Davey's private little soap opera.

Jessica and Davey stood by the table, as Angel introduced Jimmy and Greg as though she'd known them all of her life.

Greg stood up and said, "We'll move on. Not enough room for everyone. Come on,

Jimmy." Then he turned to Lauren and said, "Nice to meet you."

To Tonya's amazement, Lauren looked up and smiled at Greg. The effect of her smile on the young man must have been blinding because he stepped back, as though he'd been stunned and then turned and left, without saying another word.

Jessica and Davey said they didn't want any coffee and Angel offered them a ride home. "We won't all fit," Davey replied.

"We'll manage," Angel said. "It's almost dark and it's really cold."

"She's right," Jessica said and she and Davey followed them out of the diner and over to the Camaro.

"The girls can sit in the back," Angel said.

Tonya leaned over and whispered to Jessica, "Why am I not surprised?" Jessica smiled and shrugged.

Davey opened the back door and started to climb in. "No, you sit in front," Angel said to him.

"No," Davey answered very quietly. "Lauren will sit up there. She's got the longest legs."

Lauren didn't argue, she just climbed into the front seat as Tonya, Davey, and Jessica squeezed into the back. Angel looked furious, but eventually, she got in the driver's seat and started the motor.

The trip up the hill was entirely too fast but no one said anything. Only Jessica thanked Angel for the ride. The three girls headed off quickly, leaving Davey and Angel. As they walked toward the lodge, Lauren said, "He was nice."

"Who? Davey?" Jessica asked.

"No, the town boy, Greg. I liked him."

"You did?" Tonya and Jessica were both amazed to hear Lauren say she actually liked someone.

"He reminded me of Brian a little bit." Then Lauren sighed and said, "Of course, he was a lot shorter than I am."

Tonya, trying to keep her voice from sounding as exasperated as she felt, said, "Lauren, it didn't look to me as though Greg thought you were too tall. If you'd given him any encouragement, he would have been happy to talk to you. Why didn't you help him a little bit? I had to do all the talking, you know."

"I know." Lauren's voice was small and thin.

"You just sat there like a piece of frozen ice."

"He was sweet," Lauren said wistfully.

"Why don't you call him up?" Jessica asked. "He'd probably love to join us."

"Oh, no, I couldn't do that," Lauren answered. She seemed shocked that Jessica would even suggest such a thing.

Jessica was suddenly very tired of everyone. She said, abruptly, "I think I'm going to walk by myself for a while." She pulled her hood up, turned away from the lodge, and headed down the path toward the birch woods.

"It's cold and dark out there," Tonya warned.

"I won't go far," Jessica promised. "And it's only six-thirty."

"Don't stay out long," Tonya called. She was worried about Jessica. What was going on? Had something happened when she was out today with Davey? Tonya shook her head and reminded herself that Jessica could take care of herself. Even so, she decided to sit out on the porch for a while and wait for Jessica to come back. Something wasn't right.

Tonya brushed off the snow from one of the wooden chairs on the porch and sat down to wait. As she waited, she reviewed the day and all that silliness between Cee Cee and Lauren. Lauren's shyness was ridiculous, of course. But Cee Cee was really full of nonsense. And whatever was going on between Angel and Davey and Jessica was probably foolish, too.

What about you? a small voice asked her.

Isn't your preoccupation with Jon a little bit silly? Tonya shook her head and decided that she would take a little walk herself. She got up and walked down to the other end of the lodge and stood watching the skiers on the night slopes. Was Jon up there?

Chapter 17

Jessica breathed in the cold night air and felt her lungs begin to constrict. It would be foolish to stay out long but she really needed to get away for a while. Maybe this trip hadn't been such a good idea, after all.

She was walking in total darkness now and she knew that was foolish so she turned and stood for a moment, looking back at the lodge. Every light was on and it looked warm and comfortable.

She promised herself that tomorrow night, she would try some night skiing herself. Tomorrow night, she would know the verdict. It would all be over, one way or another. Either she would be relieved and happy and ready to really have fun or . . . well, she wouldn't think beyond optimism.

In front of her, she could see the ice on the birch trees very easily now because the light was behind them. The bare branches rustled a bit in the wind and the trees seemed to shimmer and glisten in the pale light.

What are you doing? she asked herself. Standing out here in the freezing cold, feeling sorry for yourself. Go inside where your friends are. Go on in; get out of the cold.

But she continued to stand still, listening to the distant sounds from the lodge and watching the branches of the trees dance in the wind. Today had been fun for a while. Davey was a nice kid. Sort of innocent, despite his wealthy background and jet-set girlfriend. He hadn't mentioned Angel until she showed up. Whatever was going on between them, was no business of hers.

Funny how silly it all seemed. Ever since she'd started this trip, she'd gone through the motions of pretending to worry about Cee Cee and Lauren, and pretending to be interested in Davey's music, but it all seemed so foolish.

What about you? she asked herself. What are you doing, except waiting around to find out whether you're going to live or die? Isn't that foolish? You're alive, now, aren't you?

"Yes, I'm alive now," Jessica spoke out loud to the dark night and began to walk back to the lodge with a forceful, determined stride. The crusty snow crunched underneath her boots and she was aware that she was very cold. It would be good to get inside again.

Tonya was waiting for her on the porch. "I was worried about you."

"I just took a short walk."

"But you had the flu. And you walked to the village earlier."

"I'm fine." Jessica heard the annoyance in her own voice and she put her arm around her friend and hugged her briefly. "I really am fine, you know. But cold. Let's go in."

"You're sure you're okay?"

"I'm sure." Before Tonya could pursue the issue, Jessica walked through the door of the lodge. Tonya followed and they were soon in the coffee shop, drinking hot tea and eating french fries.

"I don't think your folks would approve of the way I'm taking care of you," Tonya said.

"Too many greasy foods? Afraid they'll blame you if my face breaks out or I come home weighing two hundred pounds?"

"You know what I mean."

"Tonya," Jessica began. "I wasn't really *that* sick." Then she stopped herself. "My mom just freaked, that's all."

"You must have been a *little* sick," Tonya said. "You missed three days of school and went to the hospital."

"Just for stitches," Jessica said. She rolled up her sweater and showed Tonya her arm. "All healed, see?"

"Here comes your boyfriend," Tonya said.

"He's not a boyfriend," Jessica replied.

"Oh? What do you call him?"

"A fellow musician," Jessica turned and greeted Davey. "I was just showing off my battle scars. Want to see?"

He slid into the chair next to hers and took her arm in his hands, examining the long, red scar carefully. "What happened?"

"I got the flu and fell off a counter in the kitchen. Boring." Jessica took her arm out of Davey's hands and rolled down her sweater. "Did you have a chance to look at the music?"

"Right here," Davey said. He patted his chest. "I wanted to go over it with you."

"Not tonight," Jessica said quickly.

"But you promised," Davey said.

"I promised to sing — but not new music," Jessica said.

Tonya paid her bill and said, "I'm going to let you two musicians talk a while. See you later."

The minute Tonya left, Davey asked, "You been crying?"

Jessica smiled at how perceptive he was. He might be quiet but he certainly wasn't stupid. She answered, "I think I'm allergic to something."

"Are you *sure* you haven't been crying?" There was so much concern in his voice that Jessica was truly surprised. Maybe that was how Angel managed to hold him — maybe he was just softhearted.

"You *have* been crying. What's wrong, Jessica?"

"I can't talk about it right now," Jessica said. "I'm having some trouble at home but I don't want to spoil my trip — or the girls' trip. So I want to put it out of my mind as much as I can. Okay?"

He nodded. And then he leaned forward and put his arm around her shoulder, hugging her for a moment and saying, "If you ever do want to talk about it, I'm available. Musician to musician."

She laughed and stepped out of his embrace. "I hope I really *am* a musician. I've never performed in public."

"Not even school concerts?" Davey teased. "Cee Cee told me you won a prize in eighth grade."

"It was a blue ribbon," Jessica answered. "The kind they give to dogs or cows or something."

"Canaries?" Davey suggested.

"Okay. I'll sing like a canary," Jessica promised. "I'll wear my blue ribbon in my hair."

"I knew all along you had it with you," he teased.

She wore her blue sweater and black wool slacks with Cee Cee's heavy gold necklace and Tonya's gold loop earrings. While she thought she looked nice, she didn't kid herself that she looked as dressed up as a real entertainer would.

"We should have brought date dresses," Cee Cee lamented. "I told you all."

"I wish I'd listened," Jessica admitted. While she had been the one who was most insistent that it was foolish to bring dress-up clothes, even for New Year's Eve, she'd never dreamed of being onstage in a lounge.

"I could call my mother," Cee Cee offered. "She could send a few things up for New Year's Eve."

"No, thanks!" Tonya laughed. "There's nothing in your closet that's dull enough for me."

"I could get her to go to your mom and ask for your clothes, too," Cee Cee persisted.

Tonya frowned and shook her head. If she knew her mother, most of her clothes were already packed. The movers were coming on January fourth and her mother was well organized. "Please don't," Tonya begged.

"We look fine," Jessica said. "Everyone has on slacks and sweaters."

"Yeah," Cee Cee agreed. "Only Angel's sweaters are all cashmere and her slacks match and fit like dream pants. And have you seen her jewelry? Matching gold. Matching silver. One day at lunch, she even had on a diamond tennis bracelet."

"That's enough," Tonya said. "One — no one is trying to compete with Angel. Two — none of us have any diamond bracelets at home anyway. Three to get ready and four to go! Ready for your debut, Jessica?"

Jessica nodded and tried to smile as she said, "Ready."

"And if Angel tries to take him away from you tonight," Cee Cee said, "I'll distract her."

"Cee Cee, please *don't* try to help me," Jessica pleaded. "I'm serious."

The old Cee Cee would have made a joke or a wild suggestion but tonight she said nothing. She linked her arm in Lauren's and said, "Let's go have some fun."

Angel wasn't in the lounge at all that evening and that was a relief. During the lounge act, Davey asked Jessica to step up onstage. She wasn't even very nervous when Davey introduced her as his friend.

She really felt like his friend, too, as she stood beside him with her borrowed guitar and joined in on "Someone to Love Me." She felt calm and happy and when it was over, the audience clapped loudly.

"Isn't she wonderful?" Davey asked as she stepped off the stage. "That's Miss Jessica Mitchell and I predict that she'll be singing again soon. Maybe in the piano bar in about fifteen minutes. So come join us."

"You were great," Tonya said as Jessica rejoined the table.

Lauren added her compliments and then said, "I hope you don't mind if I go to our room now. I'm really tired."

Tonya and Jessica watched Lauren as she walked out of the lounge and Tonya sighed and asked, "Is *anyone* having any fun?"

"I am," Jessica answered. "Aren't you?"

"Sure I am," Tonya answered. But the truth was, she kept looking for Jon. What did he do when he was off the slopes? Didn't he ever come out?

"You don't have to stay if you don't want to," Jessica said. "Cee Cee's around."

They both looked across the room where Cee Cee was standing, looking eagerly at a group of young men who were huddled together talking. "Cee Cee's behaving herself," Jessica observed.

"It worked," Tonya agreed. "She's really trying."

"Here comes Angel. Time to turn in," Jessica said.

"You're not really going to let her run you off again tonight?"

"Yes, I think I am," Jessica said.

As they got up from their table, Tonya asked, "Why didn't you stay with Davey? He seems nice."

"He is," Jessica answered. "But I don't want to get too attached to him."

"You mean Angelface."

Jessica nodded. "He asked me to walk to the village with him and I accepted. But then she came along and pulled his string and he jumped. I don't want any part of anything like a triangle. Do you blame me?"

"I don't know," Tonya said. "You could always fight for him."

"No," Jessica answered very clearly. "I'm not interested."

She sounded as though she really meant it and Tonya let the subject go. But all the same, she thought if she found someone she really liked, she would fight for him. Someone like Jon? she asked herself.

She and Jessica were on their way out of the lounge when she saw Jon walking in with two of the other ski instructors. She considered turning around and going back but what good would that do? He probably thought she was a total jerk anyway.

She passed him and nodded her head. He said, "Hi," but he didn't smile.

When she'd gone about ten feet, she stopped and turned back, calling over to him, "Jon . . . Jon Baker."

He turned and she stepped up to him, saying, "Could I talk to you a minute?"

His friends moved on and he stood there, looking down at her, with no expression on his face. He was going to listen but he wasn't going to help.

"I just wanted to apologize," she said. "I was rude yesterday and it was uncalled for."

"That's all right," he answered. Then he grinned slightly and added, "At least you didn't turn me in for calling you rich."

"I'm not rich," Tonya began. Then she corrected herself, "I mean. I'm not poor, either, I guess. I mean, my dad was working in France and we took weekend vacations. That's all."

"Okay."

Jon was still smiling but Tonya had the distinct impression he wanted to go.

"Well, that's it, I guess," she said. Why did she always seem to sound so lame when she was talking to him? It really wasn't like her. "I'll see you tomorrow morning."

"I'll be there," he said.

Chapter 18

Monday

The sun was bright as the four girls rode up the ski lift. "This beats night skiing," Cee Cee said.

"Where's your hat?" Tonya asked.

"It's warm this morning," Cee Cee replied. She was willing to go along with them but a girl had to have some standards.

Jon was waiting for them with a crowd of new skiers as well as two of the men who'd shared their first lesson. He pointed Cee Cee over to the intermediate group and then he said to Lauren, "I want you to go to the expert group today."

"Oh please, no," Lauren begged.

Jon insisted. "My group is too crowded, and you're too good a skier to be here, anyway."

"But I want to stay with my friends," Lauren insisted.

"No," Jon answered, and he pointed over to the next slope.

Lauren looked at Tonya, and Tonya said to Jon, "Jon, let her stay."

"No," Jon answered. "She's a good skier and I need the room."

"Boy, you don't budge, do you?" Tonya asked. "I thought if I apologized, we could be friends."

"Being friends doesn't mean special consideration. She's a really good skier. I saw her yesterday afternoon. She looked like she was part of the ski team."

Lauren sort of hung her head, as if she had been found out and said softly, "I don't want to go."

But Jon said, "Look, that's where you belong. You'll have a better time."

So Lauren turned and left, feeling and looking to all the world like a waif.

Tonya was really angry with Jon. She was so angry that she decided that she didn't care if he was the cutest guy the world, she wasn't going to have anything to do with him. A week was only a week, and she didn't have to have a date just because Cee Cee thought everyone had to. She was going to avoid this guy like the plague.

They spent most of the next hour not looking at each other. Jon probably knew that she was angry, and clearly didn't care. All he cared about was skiing. Tonya could tell that he was one of those look-ahead, obsessed people who could be hard to get along with anyway. Good riddance to bad rubbish, as her grandmother would have said.

Tonya listened attentively as Jon gave the lesson and tried to follow his lead, but paid no attention to him personally. At one point, when no one else was listening, he asked, "Are you still mad?"

"Yes, I am," Tonya answered. "Lauren is my friend, and she's having a hard time right now."

"Well, she needs to get over it. She's a good skier."

"Her hard time isn't about skiing, Jon," Tonya answered impatiently.

"She doesn't look like a girl who has had a very hard time to me," Jon answered. "She looks like a girl who's had the world handed to her on a silver platter."

"Well, that just goes to show how much you know," Tonya snapped. "She's a girl with some pretty serious problems."

"And you're her mother?" Jon asked.

"No, I'm not her mother, but I *am* her friend."

Jon looked at her and grinned and said, "I know what kind of a person you are, Tonya. You're one of those people who always wants to make everything all right — Little Miss Fix-it."

She was furious and said, "And I know what kind of a guy you are, Jon Baker. You're one of those guys who thinks skiing is the most important thing in the world. You don't care what happens as long as you get the job done."

"I guess we've both got the other guy's number," Jon said. They looked at each other for a moment and then both of them turned away, as though agreeing that there wasn't anything else to say.

As Jon turned away, Tonya told herself, It's just a skiing vacation — it isn't as though you really liked him.

She skied down to the bottom of the hill and then rode the lift up to join the group. They were already working on knee bends and Jon had them all lined up, bending and twisting as though they were a group of chorus line dancers. Tonya took her place in line and bent and moved with the others.

As they played out their precision dance, Jon walked up and down the line, adjusting shoulders, bending knees, and straightening backs. When he came to her, he put his hands on her upper arms, just below her shoulders and said, "Twist from the waist up. Keep your shoulders straight."

She jumped from the intensity of her reaction. His hands were filled with energy — the same energy she'd seen around him that first morning. When he dropped his hands and moved on to the next person Tonya was honest enough to admit she had liked his touch very much. Get honest, she told herself. You really are attracted to him.

He let the group go shortly after that, telling them all that he thought they were a great deal better than they'd been on Saturday morning. She skied down the run without looking back at Jon, but as she skied she decided that no matter how mad she got when she was around him, she was going to try and see more of him.

He made her feel more alive than she'd ever felt and she enjoyed the electricity that he seemed to give off. She guessed she ought to admit that she enjoyed the sparks.

Next time, Jon, next time! She promised herself that she would go about things in a very different and much more controlled manner. After all, she was supposed to be smart, wasn't she?

But as the day went on and she thought

more about Jon, she realized that she didn't know exactly how to proceed. She couldn't be as eager as Cee Cee, even if she wanted to. How did you approach a young man you liked but couldn't seem to talk to? She had never had that kind of a reaction with any of the young men she knew. She was quite startled. When Jon had touched her, she'd felt as though someone had turned on all the lights. Was that what love was like? But how could you love someone you couldn't even talk to?

If it wasn't love it was something pretty special, Tonya decided. How could anyone have that kind of reaction just from touching another human being? She was in awe of her own response. She'd learned something about herself in that morning's lesson that she never would have guessed until she'd met Jon Baker.

Chapter 19

Jessica slipped out of her skiing lesson a few minutes early so she wouldn't have to talk to anyone. When she'd wakened that morning, her first thought was, This is Monday. I get the results. As she went through the morning, she discovered she was almost happy — she was so glad the long wait was almost over. She'd have lunch, and then she would call. Dr. Whitaker said he should have the results by noon. If she called at one, that would be just right. She could wait until one — she had waited this long.

Lunch was torture but she'd expected that. No matter how hard she'd tried to wear herself out on the slopes, she felt as nervous and wired as a racehorse. This is the day. She kept hearing that phrase over and over in her head.

Davey stopped by to say hello. Angel was

with him and Jessica was polite but distant to both of them. Whatever their game was — she wouldn't be a part of it.

As they walked away, Cee Cee asked, "What do you think about those two?"

"Nothing," Jessica answered.

"I mean really," Cee Cee persisted. "She's always with him but he looks at you all the time he talks to us. He's crazy about you, Jessica, I know. I've got a nose for things like that."

"I'm not interested," Jessica said shortly. "I mean it — I'm really not interested." The chicken sandwich she was eating tasted like sawdust. She pushed it aside.

"Something sure spoiled your appetite." Cee Cee looked anxiously at Jessica and Tonya and Lauren and said, "I'm sorry."

Jessica smiled at Cee Cee and said, "It's not love — it's overexertion. Long morning on the slopes." Cee Cee was on her best behavior ever since she and Tonya had squabbled and Jessica wanted to encourage peace and tranquility.

"I told you not to push yourself," Tonya groused.

"And I told you I already had a mother," Jessica snapped and then she put her hand on Tonya's and said, "I'm sorry. But I do think

I'm kind of tired. I guess I'll go to the room."

"Do you want me to come, too?" Lauren offered.

"No — you ski." The last thing in the world she wanted was anyone with her when she made that phone call. She kept her voice light as she said, "I promised to phone home today; after that I'll read for a while. Then I'm going to practice with Davey at four."

She guessed they would talk among themselves about her but she couldn't help that. If she was well, she'd be cheerful in an hour or two. If she was sick, her mother would probably make her come home. She'd think up some story to tell the girls.

She waited until exactly one o'clock to call. Her hand was shaking and she couldn't get through. After about six tries, she called the lobby and asked for help. "Sorry," the operator said. "The lines are not working in your room. But the pay phones in the lobby are fine."

"I don't want to make this call from the lobby," Jessica implored. She was counting on being alone when she heard the news — whether good or bad.

"The lines are old and they go down from time to time," the operator said. "You can call collect from the lobby."

So there was nothing to do but go down the long hallway to the line of pay phones in the lobby. Of course, they were all in the open and anyone could hear. Jessica waited until there was no one around and then she called collect.

She held her breath as she waited for someone to pick up. If her father picked up the phone, that would be the worst possible news. If her mother was together enough to answer, that would mean the new tests were fine.

It seemed an eternity before she heard her mother's voice telling the operator, "Yes, I'll accept the charges." Jessica felt her whole body flood with relief as she said, "Mom? It's me."

"Jessie, how are you?"

She managed a shaky laugh as she said, "That's what I called *you* to find out."

Her mother didn't laugh and that was Jessica's first clue that something was terribly wrong. And she kept calling her Jessie. No one had called her Jessie since she was three years old. But although her mother seemed to talk and talk, she couldn't seem to get it out — whatever it was.

"Just tell me," Jessica blurted. "Is it bad news or good?" She fought to keep the tears out of her voice.

"Don't be so cross with me, Jessie." Her mother's voice was coming through lots of tears now. "I *have* been telling you. We don't know and won't know for another few days. They haven't got any results. Oh, Jessie, I'm so worried. I want you to come home."

"What do you mean 'we don't know,' Mother?"

"I mean that the tests aren't conclusive. They want to show them to a specialist. They can't tell one way or the other," her mother said. "This is just so terrible and so hard on me. And it's so hard to be here alone. Jessie, I want you to come home."

"Mother, when will they know about the test results?" She really didn't think she could find the strength to go through much more of this. But of course, Dr. Whitaker had warned them that the labs were practically shut down during the holidays.

Her mother was crying loudly now. "We want you home, Jessie."

"When will they have the results? Do they need to do more tests?"

She could hear her mother hesitate, considering whether she should tell Jessica a lie to get her home. Finally, her mother said, "They won't know until Thursday."

"But that's New Year's Eve. That's the day

before we're coming home," Jessica said plaintively. "Can't they speed it up?"

"They say not. They say the tests have to go to Boston for the specialist to analyze. I don't understand it all. I wish your father were here. He could explain it better. Your father had to be in court. Oh, Jessie, I'm just going crazy."

Suddenly, Jessica felt angry at her mother. Didn't her mother understand that it was Jessica's problem? That she was the one standing under the sentence of death? Her mother always seemed to think only of herself.

"No, I'm not coming home," Jessica said. "I'm having a good time."

"It's so selfish of you to be up there skiing when you should be home with your family," her mother insisted.

"Mother, we've planned this trip for months. We started talking about it last Easter vacation. Every one of us saved our own money to come. I couldn't possibly come home and let the girls down in this way."

"Are those girls more important to you than I am?"

"Mother, I love you and Daddy but I want to stay *here*."

Jessica listened to her mother cry for a little

longer and then she said, "I'll call on Thursday." Then she remembered, "You and Dad will be at Aunt Lee's house. I'll call there."

"We're cancelling the trip," her mother said.

"That's silly. Aunt Lee's been planning this party for years. It's their twenty-fifth anniversary. Go to New York."

"I can't possibly go to a party when you may be . . . may be . . ."

Out of the corner of her eye, Jessica saw a group of people coming and then she saw that Angel was with them. She said, "Mother, I'm in the lobby of the lodge. I want to hang up now."

"You're not skiing all day long are you?"

"No, Mother, I'm doing exactly what I promised, skiing in the mornings, but not in the afternoons," Jessica promised.

"And you're feeling all right?"

"I'm feeling wonderful, Mother. I've told you that. I feel great. Mother, I have to go now."

"Have you told the girls yet?"

"No!" Jessica really wished she hadn't said that so loudly. The group was passing now and Angel was with them. If she'd heard any of the conversation, she didn't react. All she did was smile and wave to Jessica as she walked with her father, stepmother, and several other adults.

Jessica nodded and blinked back the tears. With any luck, Angel hadn't seen that she was crying. But she didn't seem to be having a lot of luck lately, did she?

Chapter 20

Lauren opened her book and lay down on the bed. It was good to have a little time to herself now that she was beginning to feel almost relaxed.

Jon had been right about sending her to the advanced slopes this morning. It was wonderful to be rushing down the hill. It was such a free feeling to really move on those slopes. She stretched her long legs out on the bed. She felt good all over — alive again. For the first time in a long time, she felt peaceful and contented.

Just as she was turning the pages of the book, the phone rang. She picked it up, thinking it was probably Cee Cee, inviting her to come down to the spa. A man's voice on the other end said, "May I speak to Lauren Anderson, please?"

"Speaking."

"Hi, Lauren. This is Greg McArthur, from town. Remember? Yesterday?"

"Yes, I remember," Lauren said.

"I was wondering if you wanted to go out with me tonight," Greg asked, all in a great rush of air. The whole question came in one breath. Then there was a long silence that stayed between the two of them.

Lauren's mind was racing. Her immediate reaction was to say no, and then she thought again about how she had felt at ease with him. After all, they had come up here to the mountains to have adventures.

"Yes," she answered. "Yes, I'll go."

"You will?"

"Yes," Lauren answered.

"You *really* will?"

"Yes," Lauren answered, laughing. "What time? What shall I wear?"

"Oh, wear anything. We're just going to the movies and to get pizza. There's nothing else in town."

"Will you pick me up?" Lauren asked.

"Yeah, sure. Gray pickup. I'll come for you. I'll meet you at the lodge at seven o'clock. Wait for me on the porch. Okay?"

"Okay," Lauren answered.

"See you then." And he hung up the phone.

Lauren wondered about the surprise in his

voice. Why had he called if he hadn't expected that there was a chance, at least, she would say yes? And why was he so surprised? He was a nice good-looking guy. Was it because she was taller than he was? She didn't know, but she did know that it would please her friends very much to hear she had a date.

When Tonya and Cee Cee came back, she said, "Guess what?"

"What?" Cee Cee asked. "Have you been in this room all afternoon?"

"Yes, but it's all right," Lauren said. "I have a date."

"A date?"

"Yes, a date with that fellow from town. The one I liked."

"The town boy?" Cee Cee seemed as surprised as he had been.

"His name is Greg."

Cee Cee sat down on the side of the bed, as if she were in shock. "But you didn't say a word to him. And he asked you out. Isn't that amazing."

"What's amazing?" Tonya asked crossly.

"Nothing," Cee Cee answered quickly. "I meant to say wonderful. Isn't it wonderful that Lauren has a date?" But in her heart of hearts, Cee Cee knew that she was feeling just a little sorry for herself. Life didn't always seem fair.

Chapter 21

Jessica came in and found everyone talking about Lauren's date. She went directly into the bathroom to wash her face and put some cover-up on her eyes but they were still very puffy and red from crying. She just hoped no one would notice.

She brushed her soft brown hair carefully, hoping to look good enough so that her friends wouldn't notice her eyes.

"You've got to wear more sunscreen," Cee Cee said. "What are you using?"

"None," Jessica answered. That wasn't exactly a lie. She had just washed it all off.

"You can use my number forty tomorrow," Cee Cee said. "Especially for redheads but you've got the worst burn of all of us." She cocked her head quizzically and looked at Jessica. "Maybe you should dye your hair. If you had red hair it would look natural. Maybe you really *are* a redhead and haven't discovered it yet."

"Lauren's going to wear your red sweater. Okay?" Tonya announced. "She needs something bright."

"That's fine," Jessica said.

"I'm going to the spa," Cee Cee said. "You could come with me if you want."

"I think I'll pass," Jessica said. "I promised I'd sing again tonight so I think I'll relax before supper.

That evening the three girls watched as Lauren went off with Greg.

Tonya said, "What's the program for us this evening?"

Jessica said, "I'm part of the entertainment, I guess. I promised Davey."

"What's he really like?" Cee Cee asked. "I mean, when he doesn't have his girlfriend with him?"

"He's sort of uncomplicated," Jessica answered slowly. "Or maybe I just don't really know him well. Mostly, we just talk about music."

"Aren't you even a little bit interested?" Cee Cee asked.

"I'm not interested in breaking up anyone's

romance," Jessica answered. Then she grinned, "And I'm not interested in rescue operations, either."

"There's a movie on," Tonya said. "I think I'll go see that and catch you later."

"Me too," Cee Cee said. "Even if I don't have anyone's hand to hold in the dark, I love romantic movies."

Tonya nodded and wondered if there was any way that she would bump into Jon this evening. Thinking about holding hands in the dark reminded her of that electric touch. She had felt very special when he touched her this afternoon. She would at least like to get a chance to understand that feeling a little better.

Before the movie, they were careful to order the cheapest thing on the menu in the coffee shop because Tonya had tallied up their tab and she was worried. Cee Cee had a bowl of chili and some crackers, Jessica had a cheese sandwich, and Tonya had spaghetti. When her spaghetti came, she split the second meatball three ways and shared with her friends.

Cee Cee said, "I wasn't worried about money for food because I figured we'd have lots of guys taking us out."

"You're a born romantic," Jessica said.

"Hasn't done me a lot of good, has it?" Cee Cee grumbled as she forked her portion of the meatball. "At least the movie is free. And maybe they'll have popcorn."

"I'll go with you," Jessica said. "If it isn't over by the time I'm supposed to sing, I'll just leave early. Okay?" She didn't want to get into any more long conversations with Davey. He was too perceptive.

It was a fabulous ski movie with breathtaking shots of beautiful ski resorts all over the world. The three girls watched, enthralled, and from time to time, Cee Cee poked the others and said, "We should have gone there."

As the two other girls whispered in the theater, Jessica found herself letting her mind wander away from the ski movie into the future. What would it be like if her diagnosis was a bad one? Would her life be short or long before she died? And what would she do during that time while she waited for death? Would it make her life more important, somehow? Would it make life seem more precious? Or would it just be one grinding, dismaying day after another?

She thought about a girl who had gotten sick

and died last year in school. Toward the end, she had chemotherapy and had lost her hair. She came to school wearing a wig. People were nice to her, but they treated her strangely, as though she were an alien. The whole school had sort of drawn back and watched while she got thinner and thinner and finally, one day, she didn't show up at school. Not long after that they heard she was back in the hospital and then that she had died.

Jessica hadn't known the girl that well — she was just someone who had occupied a seat in her study hall, and so she hadn't gone to her funeral. But about half the school had gone. What if it were a long, lingering illness? Would she grow lonelier and lonelier as the days went on, until finally she only had a few friends left?

Tonya, Cee Cee, and Lauren would always be her friends, but what about the others? She was glad that they didn't know what was going on with her. She'd kept her secret a secret. If it turned out that her time was short, they'd all have this memory.

She felt tears begin to flow again. They ran silently down her cheeks as though they had an independent life of their own. There was nothing she could do to stop them, so she simply let them stream down her face. In a way, it was a relief.

The lights turned on then and she felt a catch in her throat, almost a sob, and she quickly turned away. She stood up quickly, forced herself to say, "That was some film, wasn't it?" Even as she spoke the words, she was startled at how normal her voice sounded. She felt as though she could go on pretending forever. Perhaps if she pretended long enough and hard enough, she would be well.

When they walked into the lounge, Davey was singing on the stage and a woman from one of the new acts was playing the piano for him. He nodded and smiled and waved. He looked so happy to see her that she knew he'd been afraid she wouldn't come. How nice to be so young and uncomplicated that your biggest problem was whether some girl you barely knew came to sing with you.

The tears rushed back to her eyes. Suppose she didn't live long enough to experience true love? What if she never grew up and married and had a family of her own? What if this was it? No more than this. No high school graduation. No senior prom. No college degree.

In a way it was almost impossible for her to imagine. And yet she was imagining it. What if . . . what if . . .

She turned and saw a couple coming into the lounge. The woman was in a wheelchair and she looked sick. The man was older, with grayish-brown hair, and he was bending over her, looking at her face with such tenderness that it made Jessica want to cry. What if no one ever looked at her like that?

She gripped the chair in front of her and held on tight to keep from fainting. Could you really faint at the thought of never living life fully? She couldn't do that. She wanted to turn and run as far away as she could possibly run. It isn't fair, Jessica thought. It just isn't fair.

Tears threatened to overflow again and she was afraid that she might burst into hysterics in that warm, well-lighted room with all of those happy, laughing, chattering people all around her.

Davey reached out his hand and called to her. "Come on up here, Jessica."

Cee Cee began pushing her toward the stage. Jessica numbly went onto the stage and stood beside Davey. He was singing, "Bridge Over Troubled Water," and he motioned for her to join him.

Jessica didn't want to let Davey down, so she joined in on the last chorus. By the time the applause had ended, Jessica felt better.

"You're late," he said. "My part is over."

"Sorry."

"That's okay. But you'll come into the piano bar with me?"

"Thanks for sharing the limelight, friend."

"Oh, you can have some of my limelight anytime," Davey said and put his arm around her. He asked sympathetically, "Are you feeling all right tonight?"

"I feel wonderful," Jessica said. "And as long as I don't worry too much about what's coming next, I know I'll be all right."

Davey looked at her as if there was more that she had to say. But when she said no more, he hugged her again and said, "Well, let's go give them their money's worth. The show must go on."

The show must go on, Jessica thought. How long does it go on? But she did quite well the rest of the evening, joining in all the songs and helping Davey collect a large crowd of enthusiastic singers.

The evening ended late, and when the girls went back into their room, Jessica was laughing and smiling and happy. Tonya was okay, but Cee Cee was definitely down in the dumps. Jessica smiled to herself and thought, Even though I have a death sentence hanging over my head, I'm having a better time than anyone else. The world's a funny place, isn't it?

Chapter 22

The drive down the hill was awkward because neither Lauren nor Greg seemed to be able to think of much to say. Lauren was relieved when he suggested they go to the movies and then have pizza later. "There's only one show and we can just make it."

Lauren enjoyed the movie which turned out to be a ski film. She loved looking at all those world-class skiers and the scenery was breathtaking.

When the film was over, Greg said, "I hope you don't mind that it didn't have a plot. The guy who owns the theater is my cousin Horace and he's a little nuts. He thought it would bring a lot of people down from the lodge if he showed ski movies on weekdays, but the lodge shows the same kind of movies so it hasn't worked."

"I noticed the theater was almost empty."

"The *village* is almost empty," Greg said. "Not much to do around here after school so a lot of people are moving away."

"Will you?"

"I'm not sure yet. I don't think so," Greg spoke slowly and carefully as though he had given it a lot of thought.

"Anyway," Lauren said, "I loved the movie. I felt like I was right up there on the slopes about half the time. Great photography."

"Ski photography is a great thing. That's what I'd really like to do — be a ski photographer. So I come see these movies a lot."

"You've seen it before?"

"About six times," Greg admitted. "I learn something every time. Did you notice the way the camera followed that last ski team in the Alps? I finally figured out how they did it — two helicopters, not just one."

Lauren couldn't even remember which scene he was talking about but it didn't matter because Greg was still talking.

"The chief photographer was Burton Weisfoler. He's a real master. One of the first to use helicopters at all. I've seen all of his movies several times. You ever been up in a helicopter?"

"Not yet," Lauren said. "But I'd like to."

Greg frowned. "You're leaving New Year's

Day, aren't you? That's too bad because I have a cousin who's a helicopter pilot but he's on vacation till the second of January. But if you come back, you can call me ahead and I'll arrange a ride for us. Okay?"

"That would be fun." She didn't think she would be up here again for a while but she didn't tell Greg that.

"You know Burton Weisfoler is an unusual director. He does it all himself. Directing, producing, and most of the photography. He doesn't actually write the script but he plans it out in his head."

"Is he your cousin, too?" Lauren was happy when Greg laughed. Things were going well for them.

"No, but I read one of his interviews in a skiing magazine and he sounds like one of my cousins. He just ignores what people say and goes right ahead and does whatever he wants."

"A lot of people are like that," Lauren said. She was thinking of some people she knew.

Greg said, "Yeah, I guess they are. I, on the other hand, tend to hold back and check out all of the odds before I try anything. I'm a little too cautious, too tuned in to outside reality maybe."

Lauren nodded her head and then Greg

asked, "What about you, Lauren? What kind of a girl are you?"

Lauren sort of shrugged and said, "I'm quiet."

Greg grinned and said, "Yes, I can see that. You're quiet and you're beautiful. But besides that, what about you? What do you like? What's your favorite sport?"

"Skiing," Lauren admitted. "And I guess what I like best is the wintertime. I like my friends — the friends I'm up here with this week."

"But what do you do for fun? How about at school? Do you have a special boyfriend at school?" Greg asked.

Lauren shook her head quickly and said, "No. No, not anymore."

"You did?"

"I dated the same guy for two years. We just split up." She was surprised that she blurted that out to Greg.

Greg nodded and said, "It's tough to split up. I had a girlfriend for one summer and she moved to California so we broke up. For the last year and a half I haven't even taken anyone out."

"We're two of a kind." Lauren smiled. "I should be flattered."

Greg got kind of a funny look on his face

and asked, "Do you want pizza or want to try the diner? My cousin owns that, or did I tell you that already?"

He was fun to talk to. She realized that she'd never really talked to many men except Brian and her father. Greg was different from them. He was interested in things and had a lot of opinions. And he hadn't once mentioned television. That was about all Brian talked about.

I was bored lots of times with Brian, Lauren thought, and the idea absolutely amazed her. Had she spent two years with someone who bored her or was she just trying to make herself feel better?

They went into the diner and picked one of the booths over in the corner. Lauren looked around and laughed and said, "I didn't really notice it the other day, but this is right out of a forties' movie, isn't it?"

Greg nodded and said, "My Aunt Rose bought this place in 1947 and she ran it until she died about ten years ago. Then my cousin redecorated it and brought it back to its original 1947 condition and made it into a full-scale diner."

Lauren rubbed her hand across the Naugahyde upholstery on the booth and said, "I think this color is peach, isn't it?"

"Apricot. It goes with the green neon sign

in the window," Greg grinned. He continued, "Actually, everyone in our town spends most of their time trying to figure out ways to get people from the lodge to come down and spend some money. The diner does pretty well because its in the forties style. A lot of the lodge customers were born in the fifties and they like it because it reminds them of when they were young. They like it better than the antique shops."

Lauren nodded her head. "There aren't a lot of young people. Mostly middle-aged couples." Then she pointed to the jukebox in the back of the diner. "Is that an original?"

"Promise you won't tell?"

"Promise," Lauren crossed her heart.

"My cousin sold the original and bought a copy. Only a few people in my family know it. Now you're one of them."

"Does that mean you're adopting me?"

"I'd like to," Greg reached out and took her hand and said, "I really do like you a lot, Lauren. You're not what I expected at all."

"Not glamorous, just plain Lauren, right?"

"Right. Sort of an old-fashioned girl. You fit the decor in this place. This is nostalgia time." Then he asked, "Want to play a record? Do you have any old favorites? There's nothing on there before 1970."

"There's a guy at the lodge who sings a lot of old Beatles songs," Lauren said.

Greg went over to the jukebox, and Lauren followed him. They looked through the song titles, laughing out loud at some of the really funny ones. They found a group of Beatles songs and picked out two.

As they listened to the music, Lauren sipped her tea, smiled over the cup and said, "Thanks for asking me out, Greg. It's been fun."

"I was really surprised you said yes," Greg admitted.

"If you were so certain I wouldn't say yes, why did you ask me?"

Greg shrugged and laughed and said, "Can't blame a guy for trying, can you?" Then he said, "So tell me some more about you. What do you like in school?"

"I like math," Lauren admitted.

Greg laughed out loud at that and said, "It figures that I would pick a mathematical genius."

"Oh, I'm no genius," Lauren said. "In fact, I'm pretty average in school. Math's my favorite subject because when you figure out the answer and you know it's right — you know it's right. I like things you can rely on." As she said that, a stab of pain shot through her heart as she remembered that she had liked

Brian because she could rely on him.

"What's wrong?" Greg asked. "You looked for a minute as though you'd lost your best friend."

Lauren forced herself to smile and thought, Maybe I did. But she said, "Not my best friend. I was just thinking that I really do like reliable people? Are you reliable, Greg?"

"Reliable and honest, that's me," he said jokingly. "You know, I work with my dad up at the ski lodge. I'm the guy you see if you get up at two-thirty in the morning. I drive one of the Sno-Cats that flattens out the snow and grooms the runs to make them nice for the tourists in the morning. So you can count on me."

"Oh, really?" Lauren said. "I think that's exciting."

"Sure, it's really exciting to drag yourself out of bed at two or three in the morning when the weather is below freezing and roll up and down the slopes. Great fun."

"I wish it would snow while we're here," Lauren said. "Then I could see you in action."

"You could come with me," Greg offered. "It's not a helicopter ride but it's a start." Then he added, "You really can count on me, Lauren."

"Mr. Reliability." Lauren smiled at him as

she realized that for the first time, she was truly glad she had come on this ski trip.

Then the man behind the counter said, "We're closing, kids."

Lauren jumped up and said, "Oh my gosh, it's almost midnight!"

"I thought you'd never notice," the counterman said. Just as they stood up to leave, Greg's friends walked into the diner. They came over and Greg introduced them quickly and said, "We have to go now."

"Glad we caught up with you, old buddy," Jimmy said. "How are you doing?" He slapped Greg's palm in greeting.

One of the other fellows said, "We remember you, Lauren. I gotta hand it to you, Greg, old boy. I didn't think she'd go out with you."

Greg put his arm around her shoulder and they started toward the door.

One of his friends called out, "Hey, Greg, here's the ten I promised you."

"I don't need it," Greg said shortly.

"Oh, come on, you earned it," the boy shouted.

Greg hesitated a minute, but went back and took the ten dollars from his friend. Then they left the coffee shop. Greg put the money in his jeans pocket.

Lauren asked, "What was that all about?"

"Oh, he owed me ten dollars from about a month ago," Greg said and helped her into his pickup. On the way back to the lodge, they were quiet. Lauren hoped that Greg would ask her out again, but he didn't and she was feeling quite shy. She wanted to ask him out, but she wasn't sure that she felt that was the thing to do.

She began to feel nervous and got quieter and quieter. As they drew up to the lodge door, Greg turned and asked her, "Lauren, what's wrong?"

"Nothing's wrong," Lauren said. "I had a wonderful time."

Greg nodded and said, "So did I."

Sitting together in the car, they were almost the same height. Impulsively, Lauren leaned over and kissed Greg on the cheek and said, "Thanks, Greg. It did me a world of good to get away from the ski lodge for an evening."

"I'd ask you out again," Greg said, "but there's nothing to do in the village. We've done it. The ski movie runs until Friday night, and there's no place else to go."

Lauren asked, "Well, what do the kids down there do?"

He shrugged and said, "There aren't too many of us, and most of us work pretty hard. But I guess we just mostly hang around each other's houses and watch TV. It's not much to offer you."

"Would you like to come to the lodge tomorrow night?" Lauren asked timidly.

Greg smiled a big smile and said, "Wow, I thought you'd never ask. I'd love to." Then he said, "But you know, I can't spend a lot of money, Lauren. I know there're guys up there who could buy you a fancy dinner, and . . ."

"Oh, no," Lauren said. "We'll just go to the piano bar and listen to Jessica and Davey sing. We don't have to spend any money."

Greg reached over and put his arm around her. He said, "Lauren, I really like you. You're straightforward and honest."

Lauren smiled and said, "Did you think I'd be a crook?"

Greg laughed out loud. "I guess I really didn't know what to expect. More sophisticated and . . . whatever I expected, you're a whole lot better than that. I'll see you tomorrow night about seven, okay?"

"Okay," Lauren said.

And then Greg leaned over and kissed her on the lips. As his lips touched hers, Lauren relaxed and enjoyed the kiss. She closed her eyes and she said to herself, He isn't Brian but he's nice. Relax and enjoy this. And she did.

"See you tomorrow, Lauren," Greg said softly as he let her go.

She jumped down from the pickup and ran into the lodge without looking back. Tomorrow was another day.

Chapter 23

Tuesday

At breakfast the next morning, Tonya saw Jon sitting alone at a small table for two. She said to her friends, "I'll catch you later." She veered off and went over to where Jon was. She tried very hard to keep her hands steady as she held her tray of scrambled eggs, toast, and tea. She asked, "Mind if I sit down?"

Jon looked up, quite startled, and then said, "No. Sit down."

Tonya leaned back in the chair and said, "Well, I wasn't sure. We haven't been real friendly."

"Why should we be real friendly?" Jon asked.

"For one reason, we're the only two black folks on this whole mountain," Tonya answered.

"So does that mean that we have to be

friends? Is that what you're suggesting," Jon teased lightly.

"It certainly means we should try not to be enemies," Tonya said, biting into her toast. She continued briskly, "Yeah, on second thought, I think it means we should *try* to be friends. You're kind of an interesting guy, and you sure can ski. I just thought I would come over here and break the ice, so to speak."

Jon nodded his head and said, "You know, there's kind of an unwritten rule around here that the hired help isn't supposed to bother the guests."

Tonya thought about that and said, "What if the guests bother the hired help? Is that different?"

Jon nodded. "That's different. Then it's up to the hired help to decide whether or not they're interested."

"Uh-oh!" Tonya said.

"I *am* interested. I just take my job seriously. I didn't want you to think I was singling you out for any special attention. Also, I wasn't sure . . . you seemed to be pretty tight with your friends."

"I *am* tight with my friends," Tonya answered. "My friends are very nice."

"Sure they are," Jon answered, "but they're white."

"What does *that* mean?" Tonya asked. "Everyone up here is white but you and me. We just established that fact."

"But you came with them," Jon said calmly. "That could mean you aren't interested in running around with black folks."

"It could mean that I go to a school where nearly all my classmates are white. Ever think of that?"

"Okay." Jon laughed and held his hands up as though warding off her attack. Then there was a long silence. Neither one seemed to know what to say next. "Want to talk about the weather?" Jon offered.

"Blizzard coming," Tonya shot back. "I've been hearing that for two days."

"Yeah."

"Let's talk about your ski career," Tonya said. "I guess you're aiming to be a professional skier."

"I am a professional," Jon corrected her. "They pay me."

"And beyond this?" Tonya urged.

"Beyond this? As far as I can go. I'd like to believe I'm good enough for the Olympic team but I got a late start. I was fourteen when I started and that's old."

Tonya nodded. "So you're trying to catch up?"

"It's like dancers," Jon said. "The earlier you start, the better your chances, but I'm only nineteen so I've got a chance. I ski year-round now. I'm going to New Zealand this summer and I have a great coach."

"Where is your coach?" Tonya asked.

"Mount Stowe," Jon answered. "I drive up there on my day off for a lesson. The rest of the time I'm on my own."

"Why don't I ever see you around?" Tonya asked.

"I ski in secret parts," Jon laughed. "There's some back country trails that I know about. You can't get there on the lifts but the climbing is good exercise for me."

"So after you ski all morning, you ski all afternoon?" Tonya asked.

"My mornings are devoted to teaching," Jon answered and then he looked at his watch and stood up. "I'd better get up there. They'll be wondering where their instructor is." He laid a tip on the table and said, "See you later, Tonya."

"Sure." She rejoined her friends who wanted to know all about him. "He's planning to be King of the Mountain," Tonya said. She realized that she didn't know much else.

Cee Cee said, "Well, see, what did I tell you? He *is* interested in you, isn't he?"

Tonya shrugged. "He was friendly enough after I pushed a bit. Seems they have an unwritten rule here at the lodge that the hired help is not supposed to make the first advance. They can socialize, but the guests have to initiate the process."

Cee Cee said, "Well, that explains why the new lift attendant has been as standoffish as he has been."

Tonya shook her head. "Are you going to spend another day tumbling down the hill just so that guy can pick you up?"

"Oh, yes, I love the way he picks me up. He's just *darling*, you know. He sort of gets you underneath the armpits and just throws you into the seat so you won't get hit by the chairs that come swinging down. It's the most exciting part of my whole day," Cee Cee said.

As she got up to go out, Tonya called to her, "Wear your hat today. Jon says there's a blizzard coming."

"Jon says!" Cee Cee laughed and said, "Everyone says that all the time but I don't believe it. Anyway, the new lift attendant called me Red yesterday, so I know he's beginning to notice me. A cap might set me back *days*. It's Tuesday and I'm not doing too well — in case you haven't noticed."

"Wear a red cap," Tonya said abruptly. "It's

cold out there. You know you lose ninety percent of your body heat from your head, don't
you?"

Cee Cee said, "I know that when that guy
takes me in his arms and throws me to one
side, I feel warm and cozy all over." And with
that, she marched off and onto the ski slopes.

Tonya and Jessica grinned at each other and
Tonya said, "If she weren't so funny, she'd be
pathetic."

"But she is funny," Jessica said.

"She's a good sport," Lauren volunteered.
Then she said, "I guess I really did have
a good time with Greg last night because I
haven't thought about Brian all day." Neither
Jessica nor Tonya bothered to point out that
it was only nine in the morning.

"This feels different than when I used to
come here with my mom and dad," Lauren
said. "It used to seem so big."

"One hundred two rooms," Tonya quoted
the brochure from memory.

"I know we all have to grow up," Lauren
continued softly. "But sometimes I just wish
I were ten and had my mother back."

Tonya reached over and patted her hand and
said, "That's perfectly normal. I don't think
that you need to feel ashamed about that. I

think that anyone would want to have her mother back."

"Do you?" Lauren asked. "You know, sometimes I feel like such a wimp."

"You're *not* a wimp," Jessica answered. "You've got a lot going for you."

Lauren smiled. "Thanks, Jessica." She stood up just as Marshall, the waiter, walked by with a pot of coffee. While staring at Lauren, he dumped the whole pot over into Jessica's lap.

The coffee was hot, and Jessica jumped up fast, pulling the soggy wool away from her body as fast as she could. She looked down and saw her clothes were covered with coffee.

The pain only lasted a minute, but during that time Jessica felt the fear that she had been feeling all week. It welled up in her, and she felt as if she wanted to open her mouth and start screaming and never stop.

Instead, she looked down ruefully at her wet clothing and said, "I guess I'd better go change. I'll meet you on the slopes."

Marshall tried to mop the coffee off her clothes with paper napkins. The napkins crumbled into tiny little messy balls. He kept saying, "I'm sorry, I'm so sorry. Is there anything I can do?" But he was looking at Lauren while he tried to mop up Jessica.

"You could look at *me* when you talk to me," Jessica snapped. "I'm tired of your never paying attention to your job. All you do is look at Lauren."

Lauren looked as though she were going to burst into tears herself.

Tonya threw her hands up into the air and said, "Wait a minute. Let's not get hysterical here. Marshall, go get something to mop up this mess. Jessica, go change your clothes, and Lauren, wipe that stupid guilty look off your face. It's not your fault if people look at you."

She took Lauren by the arm and pulled her out of the coffee shop as she said to Jessica, "Catch up with us soon, okay?"

Jessica went to her room, threw herself onto her bed, and sobbed. It seemed as though she had carried the burden of worrying about how the tests were going to turn out for an eternity. She knew that it had only been a few days, and yet it seemed as though it had been going on for years and years. She felt as though she was a hundred years old. She was tired of feeling that way. She was tired of worrying about the future. She was tired of everything.

After she had sobbed herself out, she got up and washed her face, changed her clothes, rinsed the coffee out of her sweater and hung it up over the shower rod to dry. She changed into her other ski outfit and went out to the slopes. She spent the rest of the morning paying perfect attention to the crisp, shiny snow and what was really going on. She lived in that moment, and didn't think about the future or worry about what was going to happen next.

Chapter 24

Cee Cee was tired of flirting with the lift attendant. She'd fallen down at his feet all morning and each time, he picked her up as though she were an old sack of potatoes. When she asked him questions, he answered but he never really offered any conversation of his own. She decided to quit early.

She wished she knew what was wrong. It seemed to her that every man she talked to was either attached or leaving in fifteen minutes. Was it too much for a girl to want a little romance on her first real adult trip?

She went into the coffee shop and Marshall waited on her table. Cee Cee ordered a Coke and a cheese sandwich. It was early for lunch but who cared? Might as well make the best of things, she thought. She beckoned Marshall to come closer. "Hi, your name's Marshall, isn't it?"

"Yes." He and Lauren always seemed to be looking at the same spot on the floor. Fascinating.

"You're the guy who dumped coffee all over my friend this morning at breakfast."

"Right," he answered. And then he looked around furtively and said, "But don't mention that to anyone. They changed my station because of that, and I got a warning."

"Well, you've just got to pay a little more attention, Marshall," Cee Cee laughed, and tried to make her smile as dazzling as she possibly could. "Maybe you ought to diversify your interests, and start looking around for more than one girl. I mean, *I'm* available."

Marshall backed off and said, "You know, I'm not supposed to even talk to the guests."

"But we're old friends," Cee Cee said. "You carried our bags in that first night. You're a student?"

He nodded his head quickly.

"What's your major?"

"Marine biology."

"Weird," Cee Cee said. "You're a long way from the ocean."

"Woods Hole," Marshall explained. "I work there in the summertime and here in the winter."

"Well, tell me all about marine biology," Cee Cee suggested.

"Does *she* like biology?" Marshall asked and his face flooded a bright red.

Cee Cee shrugged and drank her Coke slowly. "I'll ask her," she promised. Might as well know when you were whipped. She left Marshall a tip and started toward her room. She was going to change into her brightest swimsuit and go to the spa. Maybe that would get her mind off her troubles.

As she walked through the lobby, she saw Davey coming toward her. He was dressed in a tweed jacket, gray sweater and slacks, and a red necktie. He looked very collegiate. Why wasn't Jessica interested in him? Angel wasn't a real obstacle.

She said, "Hi, Davey. You're all dressed up. Where are you going?"

"I've been," he said. "I had to meet some people but they're gone. Are you having a good time?"

"Well no, to tell you the truth. I keep thinking I'll run into Mr. Special, and Mr. Special is nowhere to be found." Then she smiled at him and said, "I don't suppose you're looking for a *Miss* Special, are you?"

Davey laughed at her.

"I guess you've got Angel, haven't you?"

Davey shook his head and said, "No, Cee Cee, I haven't got Angel."

Her face brightened and she said, "No? Really? Tell me about it."

"Maybe I will," Davey said. He motioned for her to join him in the lobby and they sat down together in a corner. "Maybe you can help me with this."

Cee Cee sighed. Here she was cast in the role of little sister again. It was beginning to get monotonous. But she let him talk.

"Angel is *not* my girlfriend. We've known each other for about six years because our mothers know each other. We went out on a few dates last summer, but Angel hasn't got me, and I haven't got Angel. In fact, we don't even date at all anymore."

"Well, that's not what Angel told us," Cee Cee said. "Angel said you were her boyfriend, and you do seem to hang out with her."

Davey shook his head. "I'm not her boyfriend, and I want you to tell your friends that."

"I presume you're interested in Jessica, not Lauren," Cee Cee said. "I guess that's an improvement of sorts."

"*Lauren*? Why would I . . ." He clearly didn't understand a word she was saying. He just repeated it again. "Will you tell Jessica what I told you? Make her believe it." He took Cee

Cee's hand in his and pressed it close to him. "Please, Cee Cee, I want you to help me out on this. You're a good kid."

Cee Cee nodded her head. It felt good to have someone holding her hand, even if he was dreaming of another girl. "If I help you out, will you help me out?"

"Sure," Davey said.

"Will you tell me what's wrong with me?"

"There's nothing wrong with you," Davey answered.

"I mean what is it?"

"Cee Cee, there's nothing wrong with you."

"I know it's not ladylike, and all that. But the truth of the matter is, I want a boyfriend. I want someone in my life now," Cee Cee said.

Davey snapped his fingers and said, "You mean *now*."

Cee Cee snapped her fingers and said, "Yes, now. I want someone now."

Davey said, "I'll tell you what. You get Jessica to come to the piano bar with me tonight and sing, and I'll ask a couple of guys I know who work here to stop by. Okay?"

"Is one of them red-haired?" Cee Cee asked.

"No. You don't like redheads?"

"I like redheads," Cee Cee said. "Actually, I like blonds and brunettes, too. And I'm crazy about guys with black hair. What color hair do your friends have?"

"They're both bald," Davey teased. Then he patted her on her shoulder and promised, "They're nice guys. You'll like them."

She felt a lot better about life after she'd talked to Davey. Maybe he really did have some nice friends for her. She went to her room and was surprised to find all three of her friends in the room.

Cee Cee said to Jessica, "Your boyfriend is fixing me up with a date."

"I thought you looked happy," Tonya said. "Congratulations."

Cee Cee suddenly asked, "Did you ever see that guy again — the one whose hair was exactly the same color as mine?"

"If we had seen him," Tonya assured her, "we would have roped him and dragged him home to you. Maybe you imagined him the first time."

"No, I really saw him," Cee Cee said. "He's a good-looking guy, and he's got bright red hair, kind of green eyes, not gray like mine, and he's got a real nice smile. He's about six feet tall and he wears cute little gold-rimmed glasses. He's really darling and I really saw him."

"I think you were hallucinating," Tonya

teased. "You've put so much energy into finding a guy that your mind has finally blown. It's the result of overactive hormones. Relax, Cee Cee."

"I don't have overactive hormones," Cee Cee retorted. "I have an overactive imagination. I was a latchkey child. Spent most of my childhood watching old romances on TV. And this is the result. We can't all be competent and brainy and beautiful, like you, Tonya."

Tonya said, "Well, I'm going to go work out in the exercise room to keep up my beauty. Do you want to come with me?"

"Sure," Cee Cee agreed. "I'll go with you."

Chapter 25

Jessica wasn't surprised when Davey was waiting for her as she walked out onto the porch. He was getting pretty good at finding her.

"Want to go into the village with me?"

"Sure, I could use the exercise." Jessica laughed aloud at the thought. Even half days on the slopes was a great deal more exercise than she was used to.

"I've got Madeline's car," Davey said. "We could have lunch but I promised to have it back by three."

"Oh, I don't know," Jessica said. "Where's Madeline?" She really meant, *Where's Angel?* and Davey probably knew it because he answered, "Madeline and Stewart and Angel went somewhere for lunch with some friends. They took the Lincoln."

When he saw the doubt on her face, Davey

said, "Come on, Jessica. I'll buy you a hamburger at Joe's Diner. And fries and a Coke. Or pizza. There's a pizza place in town, too."

"Pizza, then," Jessica answered. "I'll just find someone and tell them where I'm going."

She found Cee Cee first and that made it really easy. Cee Cee just said, "He really likes you, Jessica."

"I don't want any complications in my life."

"Angel isn't his type." Cee Cee grinned and added, "Neither am I. So you two lovebirds have a good time."

The Corvette was fun when you got to sit in the front seat. Jessica decided she really enjoyed the trip down the long, winding road with Davey behind the wheel. They sat quietly, enjoying the warm noontime sun and not feeling the need to say anything.

When they got to the pizza place it was closed and so they went to the diner where they found the only booth that was empty and ordered Cokes and burgers. As they waited for their food, Davey said, "My mother and Madeline are friends. She's our family's lawyer. In fact, that's how she met Stewart."

"Angel told me that your mother and her mother were best friends. She didn't tell me about Madeline. It all sounds so complicated."

"I've known Angel for years, too," Davey said. "But not very well."

"That's not what Angel told me," Jessica said quietly. Then she took a sip of her Coke and looked directly at Davey, saying, "Look, I don't know what's going on with you two but I know I don't want any part of it. Okay? You'll really have to work all this out with her, you know, not me."

"I just wanted to explain it to you." Davey seemed unsure of himself now and Jessica was irritated.

"I like singing with you," she said. "But I'm not interested in your personal problems. I don't mean to be nasty, but I'm not interested in getting involved."

Davey nodded and picked up the bill. "I just wanted to get it straight between us."

They drove back to the lodge in a deeper silence than the one they'd shared on the way into the village. As they pulled into the garage, Davey asked, "If you're going to take a walk in the woods, may I come along? I just would like to walk along with you, if it's okay. We don't have to talk."

She smiled at his perceptiveness, and said, "Yeah, maybe we could do that."

"You know," Davey said, "if there's a storm coming, you can smell snow."

Jessica laughed out loud and teased, "Are you trying to tell me you can tell whether or not it's going to snow by how the air smells?"

"Yes, I can. I learned it real fast. I'm probably good at this nature stuff. I've just never really had a chance before."

They were laughing when Angel came around the corner of the porch and called to Davey. "Davey, Dad and Madeline expect you at three. Don't forget. We're due there right now."

"I'm not going," Davey answered.

"You *have* to go," Angel said. "They're expecting you and Madeline will complain to my father, and my father will complain to my mother, and my mother will complain to your mother, and you know you have to go."

Davey stood up and said, "Okay, I guess so." He shrugged and said to Jessica, "I'll see you this evening for certain, right?"

"Sure, for certain," Jessica answered. She walked off the porch and into the birch forest, thinking, Angel sure pulls the strings whether Davey knows it or not.

Chapter 26

Cee Cee was sitting on the porch of the lodge, hugging her knees to her chin and watching the snow fall lightly. What will Davey's friends be like? Why haven't I found anyone special? I couldn't keep my own father so why should anyone want me?

Eventually, she realized she was hearing voices outside of her head. These voices were even more unpleasant than her own thoughts, and she could hear them just as clearly. They were coming from the room behind her that had a door opening on to the porch. The door was slightly open.

The words cut across the soft afternoon with a chilling clarity, "If you ask me, Angel, it's about time you started acting like a real person instead of a spoiled brat." That was Madeline talking to Angel, Cee Cee realized.

"You can't talk to me like that. I'll tell Daddy."

"Don't threaten me, Angel. I've been around long enough to know a spoiled brat when I see one. And I'm not easily bullied," Angel's stepmother replied.

"Daddy will be mad at you for insulting me," Angel said.

"Yes, he may be," Madeline replied, "but right now, I don't even care. You acted awful in front of the Redmonds and Davey and I was ashamed."

"It's none of your business!" Angel shouted.

Madeline shouted back. "You promised you'd find friends instead of trying to ruin my honeymoon. And ease up on Davey. He obviously doesn't like you."

"You're the one who doesn't like me!" Angel's voice was high and shrill. "You're a miserable woman."

"No, I'm not!" Madeline said. "I'm your stepmother."

"But you're only thirty-two years old," Angel screamed. Cee Cee was surprised at that. She thought Madeline looked a lot older than her own mother.

"Which makes me twice your age, my dear, and a whole lot more grown-up," Madeline replied. "Now, do you want me to go get your father, and we'll have it out right now, the three of us? Or are you going to apologize to Davey and find some new entertainment besides making that boy's life miserable?"

"I don't make his life miserable," Angel said. "He really likes me, he just doesn't know it."

"He really *doesn't* like you," Madeline replied. "And threatening to call his mother won't make him. Nobody likes spoiled brats."

"You hate me!" Angel was crying now. "And I hate you. Go away, just go away."

There was a long pause, and then Madeline said, "I'm leaving for now, but you're grounded until you apologize to Davey."

"I'll never apologize to him," Angel yelled. "And I'll tell Daddy what you've done as soon as he comes back."

"I want to be very clear about this," Madeline said very calmly and patiently. "As of right now, you are grounded."

"You can't ground me," Angel said. "You're not my mother. You're just someone that my father married."

"I'm leaving. I've had enough of you for today," Madeline said.

Cee Cee was amazed. In all of her sixteen years she had never heard two women screaming at each other with as much venom. She felt really sorry for Angel. On the other hand, she was glad that someone was finally telling Angel what to do. She wondered what had brought the fight on.

Before she could think much beyond that, Angel came out. She didn't even bother to apologize for the fight. She just asked, "You want to go into town with me this afternoon?"

Cee Cee thought, Aren't you grounded? But then she decided it wasn't her business. Anyway, Lauren had met Greg in town, hadn't she?

On the drive into town, Angel asked, "Where are your friends today?"

"Around," Cee Cee answered and then she pointed across the road. "Look, deer."

Angel clearly wasn't interested in the wildlife. "Did Davey and Jessica go somewhere together?"

"I don't know." Cee Cee supposed they would spend the whole trip chasing around looking for Angel's lost love. "What's so special about Davey, anyway?" she asked.

Angel shrugged. "Not much. But he *is* my boyfriend, you know."

Too bad Davey doesn't, Cee Cee thought. But she didn't say anything.

When they got to the village, Angel drove up and down the streets looking for Davey, although she said she just wanted to "enjoy the sights." When they didn't find him, Angel parked the car in front of the diner and they went in.

Three town boys were playing video games beside the jukebox and they came over to the girls' booth.

"I'm Jimmy. Did you come to town just to find me, sweetheart?" one boy asked Cee Cee.

She sighed and bent the straw on her Coke. I must be doing something wrong! she thought.

"We came to see the antique shops," Angel answered for her. "I was hoping I could find something to spend my Christmas money on."

"You could spend it on me," Jimmy suggested and then he laughed loudly.

"How about treating us to a sandwich?" the boy sitting next to Angel asked.

"Why don't *you* treat us?" Angel answered crossly.

"Can't, it's against the rules," Jimmy said and leaned back as though he'd said something really clever.

"You mean you don't have the money," Angel said.

"Let's all get separate checks," Cee Cee suggested. She definitely didn't like Jimmy and she just wanted to get out of the diner.

"Is it true your hot tub holds twenty people?" Jimmy asked.

When Cee Cee said it was true, he dropped his arm around her shoulder and moved in closer, asking in a loud, insinuating whisper, "Why don't you invite me up tonight?"

"I can't," Cee Cee answered quickly. His breath smelled of onions and she really didn't like him at all.

He moved away and asked Angel, "How about you?"

"My boyfriend wouldn't approve," Angel answered quickly.

These guys were rude and a little rough. In fact, Cee Cee was slightly intimidated by them and was scrunching farther and farther into the corner of the booth as the conversation continued.

Angel flirted with them, which surprised Cee Cee. Funny, she didn't seem intimidated at all, but she also seemed to know how to handle them. Maybe I'm not old enough to date, Cee Cee thought. It was an amazing idea and she discarded it immediately.

"Greg got an invitation up to the lodge," Jimmy said. "So why don't you invite me?" He seemed to be talking to Angel but he moved closer to Cee Cee.

"I told you I have a boyfriend," Angel answered calmly. They were finished with their sandwiches now but Angel didn't seem in any hurry to leave. She's hoping Davey will come in and see us, Cee Cee realized.

"How about you, Red," Jimmy asked as he moved even closer. "Do you have a boy-friend?"

"Yes, I do," Cee Cee answered. She wished it were true and she wished with all her heart that the date Davey was arranging for her would come through the door right now and rescue her.

"If you both have boyfriends, why are you here?" Jimmy asked.

"I told you, to go antique shopping." Angel took another bite of her sandwich.

Cee Cee noticed that she had sharp little teeth and bit into her food like rats in cartoons do. The idea made Cee Cee laugh out loud.

"I hope you're not laughing at me," a boy named Scott said. He sounded quite angry.

"No. I was just laughing . . . I just saw something funny."

"You rich girls think we're all jokes," Scott accused. "Just because Greg asked that girl out for a joke doesn't mean we're all creeps."

Cee Cee reached across the table and put her hand on Scott's. "I wasn't laughing at you, honest."

"It was a joke that he asked her out?" Angel pounced on the information.

"It wasn't exactly a joke," Jimmy explained. He seemed a little nervous that Scott had spoken.

"It was a bet," Scott explained. "We bet him ten dollars that he wouldn't call the pretty one. He did and she went out with him."

Cee Cee's heart plummeted. How was it that she was so certain that Angel would find a way to tell Lauren?

"And the rest is history," Jimmy added. He dropped his arm around Cee Cee and asked, "How about a double date?"

"You mean that Lauren's date didn't ask her out for any reason except it was a bet?" Now Angel looked like a little cat lapping up cream.

"We should go," Cee Cee said. She began to push against Jimmy who let her out of the booth rather easily.

As Cee Cee dropped her money on the table, Jimmy said, "Don't tell that girl, right? Greg would be really furious."

Cee Cee looked at him and shook her head. "There's nothing I can do to stop it."

Jimmy hit his hand against his forehead and cursed. Angel obviously couldn't wait to get out of there and tell Lauren.

They climbed in the car and were halfway

up the hill before Cee Cee tried to reason with Angel. "If you tell Lauren about that conversation, she'll be crushed and miserable the rest of the trip."

Angel just smiled.

"If you tell Lauren, I'll tell Davey," Cee Cee threatened. "You'll never catch him then."

Angel pulled over to the side of the road and asked, "How would you like to walk home?"

"I'd like that just fine," Cee Cee answered and she opened the door of the red Corvette and started the long trudge up the hill. She'd rather walk in the snow than ride with that . . . that person!

Chapter 27

Jessica and Lauren were in the spa, having a wonderful time. They'd been talking with several young people who'd just arrived and planned to stay till New Year's Eve. Among them were two fellows who Jessica hoped might be possibilities for Cee Cee. One was a high school senior from New Hampshire who skied all the time. The other one was a college-age boy who lived in California.

"Maybe you guys would like to come to the piano bar tonight," Jessica said. "I sing sometimes."

"She's wonderful," Lauren added. "My boyfriend and I will be there."

Jessica had a pretty good idea that Lauren was claiming Greg as a boyfriend partly to leave room open for Cee Cee with these guys. But she also hoped that it meant that Lauren was finally getting over Brian. And maybe she was. She'd been more vivacious this day than Jessica ever remembered.

When Angel came into the spa, Jessica was really surprised, especially since Angel usually didn't do anything that messed up her dark brown curls. But there she was, dressed in a light pink swimsuit with her hair tied up in a matching pink ribbon. Even her lipstick matched.

"Hi, guys," Angel greeted them and then turned to the new kids. "Finally!" she said. "I don't know if these two told you or not, but this place is filled with middle-aged boring."

"Angel, meet Jake and Jerry," Jessica said. "Jake is from California so you have something in common."

Angel made small talk about California for a few minutes but the way that sweet little smile kept playing around her face, Jessica was certain she was there for a purpose and that it wasn't going to be pleasant, whatever it was.

Angel turned to Lauren and said, "Cee Cee and I went into the village for lunch."

"Where is Cee Cee?" Lauren asked.

"She decided to walk home," Angel answered.

An alarm bell went off in Jessica's head. She asked, "Cee Cee is walking? Why would she do that?"

"Well, I think she got a little mad at me," Angel admitted.

"I can't imagine why," Jessica answered sarcastically.

"Don't you want to know why she got mad at me?"

"I don't think I do," Jessica said, "but I guess you're going to tell me anyway, aren't you?" She was certain that it had something unpleasant to do with Davey. This girl was really something. How had Davey ever gone out with her!

"Actually, I think it's Lauren who would want to know," Angel said, and she looked directly at Lauren. "We had a little falling-out because we ran into some of Greg's friends at the diner. They told us that Greg only asked you out because they dared him to. That it wasn't Greg's idea, at all."

Lauren's eyes opened very wide.

Jessica said, "I don't think that's the truth."

"Oh yes, it's the truth," Angel said. "When Cee Cee gets back from her walk, you can ask her. They bet him ten dollars and they stood there right beside him as he was making that call. They were really surprised that you said yes. But I told them that you didn't have any other dates."

Lauren felt numb all over. Even though they

were sitting in the hot tub, she began to shiver.

"Don't believe her," Jessica said sharply. "She's lying."

"No, she's not lying," Lauren said. She remembered that when the boys had come into the diner, one of them gave Greg ten dollars. She remembered how guilty and uncomfortable he had looked as he took the money. She was certain Greg had asked her out as a joke.

She climbed out of the tub, halfway towel-dried and pulled on her Levi's and sweater. By the time Jessica climbed out of the tub, Lauren was walking away. "Wait a minute," Jessica said. "I'll come with you."

"I'd rather be alone for a while," Lauren answered and kept right on walking.

When she got to her room, she threw herself onto the bed and sobbed. She was still sobbing when Cee Cee came in, covered with mud and absolutely furious. Cee Cee put her arms around Lauren and held her. It was obvious that Angel had told Lauren about the bet. Cee Cee rocked her as she begged, "Don't cry like that, Lauren. He isn't worth it."

"He's just like Brian," Lauren wailed. "I can't trust him, either."

"He probably didn't mean anything so bad, you know." Cee Cee was still hugging her friend but she'd stopped rocking her. "You know how guys are. They brag and fool around."

"I thought he was different!" Lauren said.

"He probably was different," Cee Cee said. Then she added, "I didn't like his friends much, though."

"Are all men the same?" Lauren asked. "Untrustworthy?"

"I don't know," Cee Cee answered slowly. "You're asking the wrong person."

"But why would he make a bet on me? I liked him," Lauren said. "What's wrong with me?"

"There's nothing wrong with you," Cee Cee answered. "You're a wonderful person. You're beautiful, you're . . ."

"It has to be me," Lauren sobbed. "It's like you read in all those books how some women just attract bad men to them. I don't know why, but it has to be me."

Cee Cee sat beside her, letting her cry and patting her on the shoulder from time to time, as though she were a baby. As she waited for Lauren to get through the worst of it, Cee Cee looked out the window into the birch forest and wondered if she and Lauren were two of a kind. Perhaps they were both doomed to failure as far as romance was concerned.

Chapter 28

Jessica waited until Lauren was gone and then she rejoined the group in the tub. As she slid in beside Jake, he said, "Your friend must be one of the most beautiful girls I've ever seen and there are lots of beautiful girls in southern California."

Jessica watched Angel's face as she heard Jake's words. Jessica said in a soft voice, "That's why you told Lauren. You're jealous."

"I just thought she should know." Angel tossed her head but the effect wasn't the same with her hair tied up.

"That's why you've been picking on me — because you're jealous of Davey. And that's why you just tried to destroy Lauren's trip. She's more beautiful than you are so you hate her. You must be a terrible person if that's all it takes to make you so mean to someone."

"I don't know what you're talking about," Angel said.

"Ever since we got here," Jessica answered, "you've been mean to all of us, and you've been especially mean to Lauren. I can understand how you might be jealous about Davey and me . . ."

"I'm *not* jealous," Angel said. "Davey is *my* boyfriend, and you're making a play for him. But you're leaving, and I'll be here, and Davey will still be mine."

"Davey has never been yours," Jessica said. "And if you don't change, no one is ever going to love you. Can't you see what you're doing to yourself, Angel?"

"I'm not doing anything to myself," Angel answered. "And I don't want to talk to you anymore." She turned her back on Jessica, moving closer to the two boys.

Jessica slipped silently out of the tub and went into the exercise room to work out. She used the machines for half an hour and then showered and dressed. She'd probably given Lauren enough time alone so it was safe to go to the room.

When she got there, both Cee Cee and Lauren were stretched out on the bed, sound asleep. They both looked absolutely miserable. Jessica shook her head in sadness and then decided that she would have to let them work things out for themselves. She had enough troubles of her own.

It was five o'clock and Jessica decided to go to the library to see Davey. She was sure he would be there practicing. She slipped into her pale blue sweater and slacks and went down the long hallway to the library. Davey looked genuinely delighted to see her and said, "Hi, Jessica. Did you remember to bring the words to that song you wrote?"

"Yes, I did," Jessica said. "I wrote them down early this morning." She pulled them out of the pocket of her trousers and handed them to him.

> Life is no breeze.
> It is a sweet song dreaming
> As the river flows on.
>
> Life is no star.
> It is a bright song lighting
> As the dream shines on.
>
> Your life and my life
> Are the same life now.
> I'll love you forever.

Love is a sweet song
Singing in the breeze.
Life is a bright star
Shining in the river.

Your life and my life,
We dream them together.
I'll love you my darling.
I'll love you forever.

Davey read the words aloud and said, "Wow, these are really beautiful words, Jessica. Did you write them all yourself?"

"Of course I did," Jessica answered. "Do you think I'd copy someone else's lyrics?"

He looked at her very quizzically for a long time and then said, "Don't take offense, but these words seem very thoughtful for a person your age."

Jessica smiled briefly. "You can't tell about people, Davey. What we see is the tip of the iceberg compared to what's really going on. People have their secret dreams and secret lives. All of us have secrets, Davey."

"And you, are you ready to share your secret?" Davey asked. "You can trust me, Jessica. And I can handle it."

He knows something's wrong. For a moment, Jessica thought about telling him about her impending diagnosis. But why burden a stranger with something that might never happen? Why not let it go until at least she knew the truth? So she shook her head and said, "Secrets are secrets. . . . How is your day going?"

He frowned. "I had a horrible fight with Angel, but I think I finally got the message through to her."

"Yeah," Jessica answered. "You got the message through, and we got the fallout." Then she told him about what Angel had done to Lauren.

Davey listened to the story with dismay, and afterward he said gravely, "There's no excuse, of course, but Angel really did have a tough childhood." When Jessica began to laugh, he held up his hand and said, "Just having money doesn't make a happy childhood. Mine's been weird, being torn between my mother and my father, but at least they love me in their own ways. Angel's mom and dad couldn't care less about her."

"Is that why you took her out, Davey? You felt sorry for her?"

Davey shook his head quickly. "Not only that. I thought she was pretty and I didn't know anyone else. But it didn't take me long to see that she was a lot like her mother. She even made the same nasty face when she didn't get her way."

"Oh, *that* face," Jessica said. "I think I saw *that* face about an hour ago. Not a pretty sight."

"I'm not asking you to feel sorry for Angel but I do. She's an emotional orphan. Nobody really cares about her."

"Except you. Maybe you *really* care for her, Davey."

Davey shook his head and looked deep into Jessica's eyes. What she saw there was honesty when he said, "No, I'm only interested in you, Jessica. You're just right for me."

Jessica laughed. "Let's change the subject."

They spent a few minutes playing and singing and then Davey said, "Let's go out for a little while."

"I think it's snowing," Jessica said. "Maybe that blizzard really is coming after all."

"Bundle up," he said and that was when she was certain that he thought there was something wrong with her health. But she didn't say anything — there wasn't anything to say.

The afternoon light was almost gone as they walked out, holding hands. "It's dark," Jessica said.

"I thought you'd like to see the stone bridge," Davey replied.

"I've seen it lots of times," Jessica was laughing.

"Sure, you've seen it, but you haven't seen it with me." Davey was leading her now and she loved the sense of being out there in the silence with another person. She could hear the snow crunching under their feet and she said, "I can smell the snow."

Soft little snowflakes fell all around them, dusting their faces and clothing. Davey leaned over and took her face in his hands and turned it up toward him. "You look pretty in the moonlight," he said.

"That's reflected light from the lodge," Jessica answered but she let her face stay tilted upward, ready for his kiss.

Davey's lips pressed against hers as softly as butterfly wings and then he kissed her eyelids, her cheeks, and her nose. Once more, he kissed her mouth. This time it was a long, lingering kiss that told her what she already knew. But she wanted to hear it from him. "What was that for?" she asked.

"That was because I really like you, Jessica. I like you a whole lot."

She was surprised how much his kiss meant to her. I've got to be careful, she thought. This is not time to get involved in a romance.

She drew back and said, "Let's keep it light, Davey. Let's just be friends."

"We are friends, Jessica." He put his arm around her and would have kissed her again but she laughed and said, "Vacation romances are fun but not serious."

He tightened his grip on her shoulders. "You know I'm not like that, don't you?"

"Of course," she answered. "Don't you know a joke when you hear it?"

"What's building between you and me," Davey announced gravely, "is no joke."

Chapter 29

Cee Cee was alone in the coffee shop when Angel came over and said, "Mind if I join you?" She had a big smile on her face.

Cee Cee looked up in surprise and said, "You have the memory of an ant."

"Oh, I remember, all right. But I was hoping you'd want to make up."

"Why would I want to do that?" Cee Cee asked in true amazement.

"Well, you look kind of lonely," Angel pointed out. "And sometimes when two girls are sitting together, then two guys come over and talk to them. Maybe we could sit here and pretend to be friends." She sat down before Cee Cee could object.

"Where are all of your friends?" Angel asked.

"Different places. Tonya's going night skiing," Cee Cee answered.

"They're all pretty good skiers, aren't they?" Angel asked. Then she raked her hand through her hair and added, "I've skied in all the best places, Aspen, Vail, and St. Moritz. This is boring here."

"I bet you can't ski at all," Cee Cee said.

Angel shrugged. "I can ski but I don't like it much. I'm not very athletic."

"So what do you do all day long in a ski lodge?" Cee Cee was genuinely curious but she couldn't help adding, "Besides make trouble and chase guys who don't want you, I mean."

"Oh, I hang around, and I talk to guys who do want me. I read magazines. I don't know." Angel really *didn't* seem to know. "I polish my nails."

Cee Cee looked at her. Every hair was in place. Her makeup was perfect and she was wearing a soft apple-green cashmere sweater, wool slacks, and suede boots to match — different than any outfit she'd worn before. "I guess looking the way you look does take time and energy."

Angel fluffed her hair again. "I went to the salon this morning. And I had my nails done. Do you like this? It's Pink Passion."

Jake and Jerry came over to their table and before Cee Cee could object, Angel invited them to sit down. Since Cee Cee was still in the middle of dinner, and she was really hungry, she didn't get up and walk away.

Instead, she watched Angel flirt with Jake and Jerry for a few minutes. When Jake asked, "Where is your beautiful blonde friend?" Cee Cee was glad she'd stayed, just to see the look on Angel's face.

When she finished her dinner, she paid her check and stood up to leave. "Don't go," Angel said. "Let's have a drink."

"Come on, sit down," Jake invited.

"No thanks," Cee Cee said and she walked away quickly before she changed her mind. It was just her luck to finally meet some decent guys and have to use every ounce of integrity she had to keep from staying. But she couldn't be that disloyal to Lauren, could she? At least I can say I actually talked to some real live college boys, Cee Cee thought. And who knew, maybe she'd run into them later in the lounge. Right now, she was going back to the room to see how Lauren was doing.

Angel caught up with her in the lobby. She touched Cee Cee's arm and said, "Oh, don't go yet. We were having fun, talking to those guys, weren't we?"

"Yes, we were," Cee Cee answered, "but talking to you isn't fun." She tried to pull away but Angel held onto her arm and practically pushed her into a chair in the lobby. Cee Cee sighed and said, "Okay, Angel, what is it?"

"I just wanted to talk. I get lonely."

"No, you don't let yourself get lonely," Cee Cee said. "You're so busy spinning your nasty little webs that you can't look at what you're really feeling. You know what you are? You're like a chocolate-covered spider. You look good, but you're poisonous."

"I just wanted to ask what Jessica's secret is."

"She doesn't have any secret. She's just nicer than you are. That's why Davey likes her better."

"No — that's not what I mean. Is something wrong with her health?"

"There's nothing wrong with Jessica's health," Cee Cee answered.

"Well then, why doesn't she ski in the afternoons?"

Cee Cee figured she'd better answer. No telling what Angel would make up if she didn't. "Her mother's kind of high-strung. I guess she worries too much."

"No, she's got a secret," Angel said. "I overheard her on the phone and I know she does. Does she have AIDS?"

Cee Cee jumped up. She thought if she

228

stayed another minute, she might hit this girl and that would really be out-of-line. "You're crazy, you know."

"There's something wrong with Jessica," Angel called after Cee Cee. "And whatever it is, it's a secret. Ask her."

Cee Cee turned and was practically yelling. "There's nothing wrong with any of us that losing you wouldn't cure. Why don't you go back to Beverly Hills and haunt those people for a while."

Chapter 30

At six o'clock, they shut down the night skiing, saying that the snow was getting too deep and there was more coming. Instead of taking the highway with the others, Tonya walked back to the lodge by way of the path through the birch forest. It wasn't very far and she could see the lights of the lodge quite easily.

As soon as she entered the woods, she felt what Jessica had described as silence all around her. Even though she could hear voices in the distance and see the twinkling white, red, and green between the spaces in the bare-limbed birch trees, she felt all alone.

It was almost as though the birch trees opened up to allow entry and then silently closed around her. She felt as though she were the only person who had ever been in these woods. The moon made the white trees glitter and the icicles hung down from their bare limbs as though they were brilliant jewels decorating an elegant woman. It was a glittering paradise.

Then she noticed that the distant voices were no longer there and that the snow was coming faster, hitting her face with more force than she'd expected. She could barely see the lights through the woods and she began to walk quickly toward them. Maybe there really was a blizzard on the way. If so, she should be inside with the others.

She wasn't frightened. She was a self-reliant person. She began to think of Washington, D.C., and what her life would be like there. Would she go to public or private school? She had the option to finish up her senior year by June if she chose. When she was with her friends, that was unthinkable, but now she began to think about the possibility of finishing early. She could go to college in the fall if she wanted. Should she?

Whatever I do, I'll be all right, Tonya told herself. She wondered if this excitement and extra fast heartbeat she was feeling could be called fear. It wasn't like her to be afraid. Where was that lodge? She should be there by now.

She forced herself to think more about Washington. Her folks would be drawn immediately into the big social whirl and she'd be alone more than ever. That was all right. She was used to that. "I'll be all right," Tonya said. This time, she spoke aloud. Her words sounded funny in the middle of all that silence. She stopped and listened. It wasn't really silence at all. She could hear the wind and she could hear the branches snapping against each other as they were whipped by the wind. The trouble was, she couldn't see very well at all anymore.

There was no more light from the lodge and the moon was obscured by the snow. Now it was very gray everywhere she looked and she began to wonder if there was a possibility that she'd gotten turned around. She believed she should only be a few feet from the clearing behind that lodge. But how could she know for sure?

She decided the best thing to do was keep on walking in the direction she was headed, even if the direction was wrong. These woods were just a few acres, and soon she'd be out on the street. It wasn't possible to get very lost this close to home, she was certain of that.

But you read about these things all the time, Tonya heard a frightened little voice in her head. People fall and drown in two inches of water. People go out for the mail and freeze to death because they locked themselves out of the house. "People do but I don't," Tonya said very loudly.

As she walked, she was aware that the wind was very sharp and very cold. The trees should be breaking the worst of it but it was very strong. Ice pelted her face, like thousands of tiny sharp daggers. She wanted to keep her head low but she was afraid she would miss any signs of light. She was glad she had her goggles on, otherwise she would be in real trouble. You *are* in real trouble, that voice said again.

Now the wind sounded as though it were screaming and Tonya was holding her hands up against her face to beat away the sharp, hard, jagged pellets of ice. It will be over soon, she told herself and tried to imagine the lobby of the lodge with the giant fireplace and all those television sets going full blast.

She turned and looked backward. Should she turn around? Was she going the wrong way? The ice and snow were beginning to cover her footprints. Not only was she dealing with the darkness, but she also was dealing with the fact that the new whiteness of the night storm was covering up her tracks. Should she try and leave signs? There must be a ski patrol somewhere. Maybe her friends had already reported her missing. Maybe.

She laughed aloud as she realized that she had done exactly what Jon had warned them all about, that first day. Lauren's father had made her promise to take care of the others — but she was the one who had put herself at risk. It would have been funny if it weren't so pathetic. Tonya wanted to cry but she knew it would simply fog up her goggles. Better keep a clear head.

She reached up and snapped a twig off one of the birch trees and carefully laid it on the ground so that it was pointed in the direction she was walking. Then she began turning slowly all around in a 360-degree circle, looking through the trees for some sign of light. When she couldn't see anything, she took off her goggles and blinking back the pelting ice, forced herself to turn again, carefully observing the darkness.

She stopped, holding her breath as she thought she saw a light. It seemed to be bobbing and then she saw another light beside it. The ski patrol!

"Over here!" she called.

The lights began to move closer and she breathed a sigh of relief. They had heard her. They were coming to rescue her. It was going to be all right.

A light shined in her eyes and she smiled. "Am I glad to see you guys."

"Tonya!" It was Jon's voice and he was clearly angry.

For just a moment, she wondered if she might be hallucinating but the voice was too real and the anger was too close to the surface for a dream sequence. It was Jon all right and he wasn't happy about finding her.

She wanted to turn and run but she didn't. Facing Jon's disapproval was better than freezing to death, but not a lot.

"Jon, I'm over here." She tried to keep her voice well modulated and without fear.

Jon came crashing through the woods. He grabbed her arms and hugged her tight, then he asked, "Are you all right? Are you hurt?"

"Of course not, I just took a walk," Tonya answered.

"Just took a walk? Are you crazy?" Jon lowered his voice on the second question because other men came up behind them.

"No, I'm not crazy. I just wanted to walk in the woods."

He turned to the other two men and said, "I'll take her in." He put one arm around Tonya and used the other hand to flash light onto the ground in front of them. He asked, "Can you walk all right?"

"I *was* walking," Tonya pointed out. But she was really was glad to see him and she loved having his arm around her. He might be angry but he was someone to lean on and she was tired.

"Well, you can walk with me now," he said. He kept his arm around her shoulder and pushed her through the woods as quickly as he could.

As Tonya had guessed, they were not very far from the lodge. It took only about fifteen minutes to get to the clearing behind the lodge. When they stepped out of the woods and into the open, well-lighted space, she said, "See, I knew there was nothing to be afraid of. I knew I was close."

He frowned at her, grabbed her by the shoulders, and shook her slightly as he said, "People die doing damn fool tricks like that. You should have known better."

She said, "I almost didn't answer you. I knew that you would be mad at me."

He looked startled and said, "Of course I'm mad at you. Why wouldn't I be mad at someone who deliberately endangered her own life? You girls!"

"Don't say 'you girls' in that tone of voice to me, Jon Baker," Tonya said. "I won't be lumped with every other woman that you've met up here on this mountain."

He laughed shortly, pulled her closer, and kissed her hard on the mouth, then said, "No, you're different. Everything about you is different. Aren't you afraid of anything?"

She was startled by the kiss and stepped back, opened her eyes wide. "You can't kiss me like that."

"Like what?" he asked.

"Why did you kiss me? I didn't say you could kiss me."

"Well, I thought I deserved a kiss." He was grinning now. "After all, I rescued you from the woods."

"You didn't rescue me from the woods," she said. "I was perfectly fine. I wasn't lost, and you shouldn't kiss me unless you have permission."

He laughed and said, "If I waited for permission, it would be a long wait. I'm beginning to figure you out, Tonya." And with that, he pulled her into his arms, held her close, and kissed her again.

Her legs felt strange and she thought she might get dizzy from the reaction she had to being kissed by him. This is ridiculous! she thought. She pulled away and said, "I'll decide who I want to kiss and when I want to kiss them."

"Whom," Jon teased. "You should say *whom* I want to kiss. I thought you were the smart one."

She turned and walked away from him, moving as quickly as she could toward the lodge. He called after her, "I take it back about not being afraid of anything. You're afraid of me, aren't you?"

Tonya began running. She was aware that her reaction was not a logical one, but it was her reaction. She didn't like him being angry at her and thinking she was in danger when she wasn't in danger. He was way off-base, she told herself. But most of all, she hated hearing his laughter rolling behind her as she ran inside.

Chapter 31

Lauren waited in her room until the phone rang and when she answered it, Greg said, "Lauren?"

"Yes."

She could hear Greg's voice very clearly so that meant he *did* drive up in the blizzard. "I'm here," he said, "but I couldn't find you in the lobby."

"No," Lauren said, "I'm not in the lobby."

"What's wrong? Did you forget we have a date?"

"No date," Lauren answered. There was a pause and then she said angrily, "You asked me out on a *bet*."

"I should have told you myself. But Lauren, just because I asked you out on a dare doesn't mean I didn't want to ask you out."

"What it means," Lauren said, "is that I can't trust you. Go home, Greg."

"Look Lauren, I drove a long way in a snow-storm. Couldn't you just come down for a minute? We could have some coffee and talk about it?"

"No," Lauren said. "I don't want to talk about it."

"Well, I don't really know that that's fair," Greg began.

"It's fair," Lauren said, and she hung up the phone. She turned and stared at herself in the mirror. Hugging herself close, she looked in the mirror at the tall, blonde, beautiful woman who stared back at her. She felt as though she were looking at a stranger. It was as though she didn't know herself, didn't know herself at all. She wondered who she was. First Brian and now Greg.

"Who am I?" she whispered. But there was no answer from the mirror. Then the lights began to flicker and dim and then they went completely out. Lauren waited for a moment, expecting them to go on again, and then she remembered that there was an emergency candle by her bed. She felt her way along the wall until she found the candle and the matches. Then she went and sat in a chair in the dark, staring at the candle.

After five minutes, the lights still had not come back on, and Cee Cee and Tonya came into the room with a lit candle. They said, "Lauren, you can't sit here in the dark all night. Davey says this could go on for a long time. You'd better come downstairs with us."

"Has Greg gone?" Lauren asked.

"Yes, he left right after he talked to you," Cee Cee said. "He won't be back, judging by the look on his face."

Tonya said, "You were a little rough on him, you know. I think he really likes you."

"I don't want anything to do with anyone I can't trust," Lauren answered.

"Just because he asked you out on a dare doesn't mean you can't trust him," Cee Cee began.

But Tonya poked her friend and said, "Don't worry about that tonight. You just can't sit here in the dark all alone. Come into the lounge with us."

"I'd rather sit in the dark," Lauren said.

"It's not good for you," Tonya insisted.

"It's not fun either," Cee Cee added. "Come on! Davey rounded up these two guys for me but they're talking to each other. These ski bums really don't care about anything but how deep the powder is. If I've heard one story about their fancy equipment, I've heard a hundred. Do you know ski boots can cost five hundred dollars?" Cee Cee made a face. "And when I asked for a second Coke, the guy acted like I'd taken his last nickel."

"I don't want to talk to strangers," Lauren said.

"Don't worry," Cee Cee assured her. "They'll talk to each other whether you want to talk to them or not."

Lauren knew that her friends would stand there and argue in the flickering candlelight until they forced her into the lounge. She asked once again, "You're sure he isn't there?"

"We're sure. We wouldn't lie to you," Tonya assured her. They walked down the long hallway, carrying candles. The flickering lights threw weird patterns on the wallpaper and Cee Cee said, "Maybe my red-haired guy really is a ghost. Maybe this is the night he'll come out of the wallpaper again."

When they entered the lounge, there were triple candles on every table and the fireplace was throwing off a lot of light so the room had a wonderful festive glow. They joined Davey's two friends at the table and watched as Jessica and Davey finished their last song. Davey put his arm around Jessica and she let it stay there.

"Looks like love," Cee Cee said with a sigh. The two guys Davey had introduced her to hadn't even bothered to look at Lauren. They really were interested in their conversation!

Jessica and Davey joined them and they all went into the piano bar where they sang while the help ran around, trying to get the alternate generator going. By the time the generator went on, the candles had burned down to a nub. When the lights went on, people seemed almost disappointed and someone immediately dimmed the switch.

"I think candlelight is so romantic, don't you?" Cee Cee said to the two fellows.

"Sure," the taller one answered. Then he asked, "You want to dance?"

Cee Cee said, "Yes, of course," and slid off the bar stool. Davey started playing a fast song and sang the lyrics. His friend, Ted, turned out to be a pretty good dancer and Cee Cee had a good time moving to the music. When the dance was over, he took her elbow and led her back to the piano bar. This is more like it, Cee Cee thought. Ted turned to his buddy and asked, "You thinking of getting some of those new Hallekuis?"

"Expensive," his buddy replied. "That's a lot of money for snow tires, even if they do come from Norway."

"How much is too much?" Cee Cee asked. She wondered if they cost more than the guy's boots.

"Six hundred," he answered.

"That's more than your boots," Cee Cee chimed in.

He stopped and looked at her as though he was trying to figure out what she was saying, and why. Finally, he said, "Guess I'll turn in. Powder tomorrow, if this stops."

They both left at the same time and Davey looked at her and shrugged a kind of apology. Cee Cee raised her hands and arms in a "what can you do?" gesture and chewed on the lemon rind at the edge of her 7UP.

One older man asked Lauren to dance and she shook her head and looked at the floor. "Come on," he insisted and took her arm.

Lauren jerked her arm away and said, "No, thanks." Then she said, "I'm going back to the room now."

"I'll go with you," Tonya said and the two of them were out the door.

Cee Cee sat alone at the bar, chewing on her lemon rind, wishing something wonderful would happen to her. Something wonderful was obviously happening between Davey and Jessica. Why not her? At least she wasn't jealous of Lauren anymore, she told herself. Cee Cee could actually say that since she'd seen the way Lauren was so crushed by Greg's bet, she hadn't had even a twinge of jealousy.

She decided she would try to be as elusive

and noncommittal as Lauren was. Obviously, she was trying too hard. She struck an elegant pose, tipping her head up and stretching her neck about three inches longer. She waited as calmly and patiently, and silently, as Lauren did. But nothing happened.

Chapter 32

Wednesday

Tonya was up before anyone else in the morning so she dressed quietly and slipped out of the room. It was too early to ski but there wasn't any sense in sitting in her room. A cup of tea would be good, she decided, and she hoped the dining room really did open at six-thirty.

It was open and Jon was the only other customer. He raised his hand in greeting and motioned for her to join him. How could she refuse?

She wondered what he had to say after last night. But Jon acted as if last night had never happened. He talked about the big storm and the powder conditions that would be available this morning and he looked pretty enthusiastic as he talked. "I'll show you some different places to ski, okay?" he offered. "Places that aren't on your map."

"Can you do that?" She decided she would never understand him. How could he sit there so coolly and talk about new-fallen snow? Didn't he remember the way she had felt in his arms? Didn't he feel the same electricity when they kissed?

He finished breakfast and asked, "Why don't you meet me at eleven and we can ski together?"

"You never smile when you talk about work," Tonya observed. "Do you really like to ski? Is it fun for you?" Jon was standing right beside her. She could reach out and touch him if she wanted to, but — but that would be silly. It was seven o'clock in the morning and he wanted to talk about skiing.

"Fun? Not exactly. It's more like a passion," he answered, and then he grinned. "Listen, I take my work seriously. I'm a serious kind of guy. You should have figured that out by now, Tonya."

"I figured it out," Tonya answered. "And if I weren't on vacation, I might even like it. But I keep looking for you and you're never around. I thought you might have come into the lounge last night. Where were you, Jon?"

"Nothing mysterious. Mostly I'm tired and I crash early. Or I'm in my room reading." Then Jon admitted, "I've never even tried to fit into the social scene around here."

"There isn't any social scene," Tonya said. "You should talk to Cee Cee about that."

"Cee Cee is what I'm talking about — girls who come up here for a weekend or a week and leave you behind with a broken heart. I've seen more of that than I care to," Jon said.

"So is that what happened? You got your heart broken?"

Jon laughed at the idea. "Nope. I just take care, that's all."

Tonya was beginning to get angry. Jon was both opinionated and evasive. "Then why are you talking to me now? Why did you invite me to go skiing with you?"

"Why indeed?" Jon stood up, glancing at his watch and said, "Don't keep me waiting, Tonya. Eleven o'clock at Devil's Run."

Then he bent quickly and kissed her on the cheek, saying, "I get a little self-protective when I'm working and everyone else is on vacation. It's a weird experience, but when I meet someone I really like, that should be different, shouldn't it?"

Before she could answer, he was gone.

She and Lauren skied on the new snow all morning and it was a glorious experience. There was something so beautiful about all that fresh whiteness that Tonya felt as if she wanted to stay on the slopes forever. "I could really get to like this," she confided to Lauren.

"Let's see if we can get jobs here next Christmas," Lauren said. "Maybe be waitresses on the evening shift and ski in the mornings. We'd do better than Marshall."

Tonya laughed. "Anyone could do better than Marshall." She didn't want to talk about next year right now. Washington, D.C., was too far away from New England. Besides, every young skier dreamed of getting a job on the slopes. Even the good ones like Jon settled for second-rate resorts like this one. Lauren and Tonya probably didn't have a chance.

"You don't think that's a good idea?" Lauren asked.

"Let's talk about it tomorrow," Tonya said. "I've got a date with Jon to ski the back country." When she saw the longing in Lauren's eyes, she asked, "Want to come along?"

"No thanks," Lauren answered. "I'm practicing my carving on this slope until I'm perfect."

She was waiting at the top of Devil's Run at five minutes to eleven when Jon joined her. He took her hand and said, "Come on. I'll take you on a tour."

"I've already skied this slope several times.

It's no harder than Indian Run, just longer," Tonya answered.

"But you haven't been down Tower Run, have you?"

"There isn't any Tower Run."

"There is today." Jon pushed off with his skies, calling out to her, "See if you can keep up."

Jon led her partway down Devil's Run and then he made a sharp left over a slight ridge and behind some big rocks. Tonya followed him but she wasn't sure what he was up to. When she got around the corner, he was waiting for her.

"Wow!" They were in a small, unmarked valley that Tonya hadn't even known existed. Below them, lay the longest, smoothest slope that she'd ever seen. She asked, "Is this for real?"

"Not quite," Jon answered. "You'll have to follow me exactly because there are some really big rocks under that white stuff."

"Uncharted territory?"

"I have the charts here." He pointed with one gloved finger to his head. "This is a secret slope," Jon answered. "Not on any of your maps and only the regulars know about it. See? There're no tracks at all."

"It's beautiful," Tonya said.

He took her hand and they looked out over the valley into the higher mountains beyond them. "That's Mount Washington over there," he pointed. "Highest peak in New England. I'll be skiing that next week."

"Now that there's real snow," Tonya added.

"Now that there's real snow, we've got lots of options," Jon said. "Today, we'll ski Tower Run."

"Where's the tower?" Tonya asked.

"You'll see." Jon pulled out ahead of her and called back, "Don't be scared, just do exactly what I do."

"I hope that doesn't involve somersaults." Tonya was only partly kidding but she followed Jon, staying as close to his ski tracks as she possibly could. It was a little scary knowing she was skiing on uncharted territory but it was also fun. She trusted Jon and she tried to do exactly as he did.

The slope was a gentle easy one and she was comfortable for about five hundred feet. Then she saw Jon suddenly lean to the left and turn his skis in a sharper turn than she had ever tried. Her heart began to beat faster and she knew she was scared. What if Jon had misjudged her ability? She took a deep breath and leaned as she'd seen him lean, making the turn with the top of her body first, staying almost on top of his tracks.

After she made that first turn, she felt she could do anything. She relaxed and looked out at the wonderful panoramic view of the whole valley below. Mount Washington was in the distance and there was even a frozen lake surrounded by pine trees that she didn't know existed. The lodge was behind them and the village was even farther to Tonya's left than on any of the other runs. She realized there was a rock building below, which she'd never seen before. Was that the tower?

But following Jon down the slope was enough of a job without trying to look at the scenery. It was a long, smooth glide for hundreds of feet and she loved the feel of the wind against her cheeks. This is the way skiing is supposed to feel, Tonya told herself. She was honest enough to admit that part of the feeling was because she was following a great skier. Jon's bright blue jacket looked like a sailboat flying across the sea, now. He was going pretty fast and Tonya decided she wouldn't try to keep up with him. No sense breaking her neck just to try and impress him.

He was waiting at the bottom of the slope when she got there and he asked, "How about that for a run?"

"It's great!" Tonya replied. "It's too bad they can't have it open year-round."

Jon nodded. "There's a rumor that some businessman is thinking about putting twenty or thirty million into this place. Build condos. Add more runs and lifts. Make it one of those McDonald's Resorts that are all over the place."

"I'll bet I know who the businessman is," Tonya said. She was guessing it was Angel's father. "But I don't even want to think about that today. How do we get back up to the top?"

"We can't," Jon said.

"Then how do we get to the lodge?"

"We have some hiking to do," Jon admitted. "But first, let me show you the tower."

She slipped out of her skis and when Jon offered to carry them for her, she said, "No thanks." It was a short distance but a difficult journey across the flat snow. Each step she took, she sank into about a foot of new snow. As they neared the tower, the ground grew icy and Jon took her hand.

Tonya realized they were walking around the edge of the birch forest and she asked, "How far are we from the lodge?"

"About three miles," Jon answered. "We're on the other side of the forest. We'll take a tour of the tower and then I'll buy you some lunch."

As they walked, Tonya felt warm and close and comfortable. Right now, it was as if she had known Jon all of her life. It had been an absolutely marvelous morning. But she couldn't help wondering what came next. Would Jon buy her lunch and say good-bye? Or was Jon really interested in getting to know her? Could he guess how she felt when she was around him? Did it show?

"This is the famous tower," Jon said and he pointed to a tall, round building made of gray rocks. There were places where the walls were covered with the skeleton of a vine and there were places where the stones seemed to have fallen away completely.

"Who built it? And why?" Tonya asked.

Jon slipped his arm around her and said, "The story is that back in the twenties, some rich man had a wife who loved to ski. He built it just so he could have a place to write while she skied. But they got a divorce. So I guess no one's ever really lived there."

"But someone must own it," Tonya insisted. "Why don't they take care of it."

"It isn't worth anything anymore," Jon answered. "No one could live in it. Just a good place for sweethearts to meet and be alone. Want to go inside?"

"No," Tonya answered. "I don't think we'd better."

"It's all right," Jon said. "Come on." He took her hand and drew her through the open door. They walked into a room with a fireplace and some boxes to sit on. There were stone steps that led to a loft high above them.

They climbed to the loft and Tonya looked out the window at the forest and asked, "Do we have to walk through those trees to get back to the lodge?"

"We can walk around the woods," Jon answered. "But going through the forest is the fastest way.

"Look over there." Jon pointed out the window on her right. As he pointed, his arm circled her and she was certain that he would take her in his arms and kiss her. How did she feel about that? She wasn't sure. Nervous, for sure. She couldn't really think very well when he stood so close. His breath was warm on her cheek. She didn't move. "If it doesn't snow anymore, I'll take you skiing tonight."

"Why do you think it might snow again?" Tonya asked. Her words had trouble finding their way out of her throat.

"Instinct. You develop an instinct about the

weather after a while." Then he looked down at her and said, "We'd better get back before you freeze."

He turned and she followed him down the stairs. They made their way to the road and started walking. About five minutes later, a woman stopped and offered them a ride and they took it. So they were back in the lodge coffee shop having lunch before the snow actually started.

After lunch, Jon said, "I'll pick you up around six if the snow has stopped. Night skiing, okay?"

As they parted, he reached up and touched her cheek with his hand and said, "It was great fun. See you tonight."

Tonya said nothing but she couldn't keep from wondering. If it was so great, why didn't you kiss me?

Chapter 33

Cee Cee was waiting for Tonya at the lodge. She said, "Lauren and I have been talking and we think we ought to talk to you, too."

"What's up?"

"I didn't want to mention it last night but something funny is going on. Either Jessica lied to me this morning or . . . I don't know."

"Why would she lie to you?" Tonya asked.

"I don't know," Cee Cee answered, "but when I asked her if she wanted to have lunch with me, she said she was going to meet Davey for a picnic."

"That's normal," Tonya said. "Haven't you seen the way they look at each other?"

"Yeah, but what's not normal is that when Lauren and I had lunch, Marshall waited on us."

"What did he spill?"

"Just a little soup. But he said that Davey

drove into Manchester early in the morning to get decorations for the New Year's Eve party."

"So either Jessica had a date with someone else and didn't want to tell you. Or there was a mix-up and she'll be back soon. Or she wanted to be alone." Tonya was secretly inclined to think that it was probably that she wanted to be alone.

"That's not all," Cee Cee said. "Angel says she's certain that Jessica has a big secret."

"You're not hanging out with Angel again?"

"And you know, she is acting peculiar — Jessica, I mean."

"I don't think she's acting any more strangely than some of the rest of us," Tonya said.

"I always act strange," Cee Cee brushed aside the comment. "It's my M.O. But, ordinarily, Jessica is a solid citizen. What do you think?"

"Maybe she just wanted to be alone," Tonya said. "We *have* been living in cramped quarters."

"I'd be willing to bet that she really does have a secret," Cee Cee said. "And I think you ought to do something about it."

"That's silly," Tonya answered shortly. "I'm

going to go to the exercise room and work out. Want to come with me?"

"For a little while," Cee Cee said. "Then I'm going to find Jessica."

Lauren wanted to go back to the slopes and both of her friends were happy that she was willing to go alone. As she walked away, Tonya said, "I think Lauren's finally getting over Brian."

"Now if she can just get over Greg," Cee Cee said. Then she laughed and added, "I think I'm getting better, too. I actually enjoyed skiing this morning and didn't waste all my time looking for guys. Having those two losers for dates last night probably cured me."

But when they got to the exercise room, Cee Cee broke away from Tonya and immediately struck up a conversation with some young men who seemed happy enough to talk with her.

Tonya worked out, running on the treadmill and using the barbells before she got on the Stairstepper. If she was going to keep up with Jon, she'd need to get in a lot better shape. And she was pretty sure that she wanted to keep up with Jon as long as she could. This evening, when they were on those slopes in the moonlight, she was going to order him to kiss her again. It seemed like the only way to deal with the overwhelming need she had to touch him.

As she worked out, she thought first about Jon and then she admitted to herself that the talk about Jessica's secret upset her a lot. First of all, she thought Cee Cee might be right and Jessica might *really* have some kind of secret. Maybe her folks were getting a divorce. Or maybe it was something else — maybe there really was something wrong with her health.

We all have secrets, Tonya reminded herself. She had one of her own and soon she would have to share it with all her friends. As long as she'd been on this trip, she'd been successful at not thinking about her impending move. But in a few days, they'd be going home and she'd have to face the inevitable.

She would miss them all. Lauren and Jessica, of course. But in a lot of ways, she would miss Cee Cee the most. Cee Cee made her laugh and that was a wonderful quality. When I'm saying good-bye, I must be sure and tell her that, Tonya thought.

In a way, it felt like she was cheating when her friends said something about the future. When Lauren talked of getting a job at the lodge next year, it was as if little slivers of ice lodged in her heart. Yet, she might come back sometime — especially if Jon was here.

He won't be here long, she warned herself. He wants to go to New Zealand this summer. The knowledge cut into her anticipation of being with him this evening. What was it Jon said about girls who left you and broke your heart? What would *he* do to *her* heart?

Tonya left the exercise room, showered, and slipped into the tub beside Cee Cee. "You look great in that swimsuit, Tonya." Cee Cee was sitting alone in a chair next to the hot tub. "You should invite Jon to join us tomorrow," she said.

"Apparently, Jon's not very social."

"He looks pretty nice," Cee Cee continued with a mischievous glint in her green eyes.

"Yes, he *is* nice," Tonya said.

"I mean he's *really* nice, Tonya. He might be someone to hang onto. He'll be up here all winter. Maybe he'd like to come down to Danbury for a visit. We're only four hours away."

"Yeah, maybe so." Tonya slid into the water up to her neck and stared at the ceiling. "Ever notice that mural?"

"I've got it memorized," Cee Cee assured her. "You could ask Jon to come down for the first basketball game," Cee Cee offered.

Tonya flapped her arms and tossed water at Cee Cee. "Don't make any plans behind my back. Let me make my own plans."

Cee Cee shook her head and said, "I know you pretty well, Tonya, and one of the things I know about you is that you're not really into nailing down the future. You'll let Jon go by default."

Tonya laughed and answered, "You can't always tell what's going to happen in the future. It's better to live life one day at a time."

"Oh, I don't know, I kind of like to arrange things," Cee Cee answered.

Tonya looked at her speculatively and said, "You do, don't you? Why don't you go into management. Or you'd probably be a good teacher."

"Me? I'm not much of a student," Cee Cee said.

"But you're real smart, and real imaginative," Tonya answered. "You'd be a good writer, if you put your mind to it."

"Hah," Cee Cee said shortly. Then, changing the subject she said, "You want to help me find Jessica?"

"No. People are entitled to their private lives."

"Tonya, do you think there could be anything really wrong with Jessica?"

Tonya answered thoughtfully. "I don't think so. She always seems healthy to me."

"Then why isn't she skiing in the afternoon?" Cee Cee asked. "Angel asked if she had AIDS, but Angel is a witch. She could have though, couldn't she?"

"She doesn't have AIDS," Tonya said. "That's stupid."

"But she was in the hospital once. Maybe they gave her transfusions and . . ."

"You should write soap operas," Tonya said shortly. "And leave real people alone."

"Maybe we ought to try to find out what's really going on," Cee Cee said. "You know, to protect her from Angel, if nothing else."

But Tonya, who had a secret of her own, shook her head and said, "I think when people have secrets they should be allowed to keep them, don't you?"

Cee Cee didn't know, and she said so. Tonya reached over and patted her hand and said, "Honey, I know you're not having a real good time on this trip, but you've got such a tremendous amount of energy and you always have the ability to have fun. Why don't you just sort of buck up and enjoy yourself? Forget about romance, and just have fun skiing like the rest of us."

Cee Cee looked at her and said, "Well, you say you're having fun skiing, but I saw you holding hands with Jon this morning."

Chapter 34

Cee Cee found Marshall in the coffee shop and quizzed him again. "You sure you haven't seen Davey?"

"He went into Manchester early, just like I said, to buy decorations," Marshall replied.

"And Jessica didn't go with him?"

Marshall looked shocked. "Oh no. Mrs. Burton, the owner's wife, went with him. He wouldn't take a girl."

Cee Cee shook her head and stirred her chocolate with a spoon. There was something very funny going on. Why had Jessica been so certain she was going to meet Davey when she left this morning?

She looked at her watch. It was almost three and Jessica still wasn't back. If Tonya wouldn't help her, she would have to get to the bottom of this herself. She asked Marshall, "Have you seen Angel anywhere?"

Marshall shook his head and blushed. Cee Cee realized that he had a stock response to any pretty girl's name. Poor guy. He had some work to do.

She left the coffee shop and walked down the long hallway to Angel's suite where she knocked on the door. Angel answered and she asked, "Have you seen Davey today?"

Angel had a little smile that played about the edges of her face. "I believe he's gone into town today."

"For the whole day?" Cee Cee kept her voice as light and disarming as possible.

"For the whole day," Angel said nonchalantly. And then she asked, "You want to go into the village with me later on this afternoon?"

"Maybe so," Cee Cee answered. "Have you seen Jessica?"

"No, I don't think so."

She's lying. Cee Cee was certain of that. But she decided to outsmart her. "I was hoping you had," Cee Cee said. "Maybe I'll look for her in the woods. She likes to walk."

"Do that," Angel said smoothly.

She's not there, then. "Or over at the tower."

Angel's face remained impassive except for that tiny little smile that seemed to have a life of its own. The trouble was, Cee Cee didn't exactly know where the tower was. "Maybe you'll help me?" Cee Cee said.

"Help you what?"

"Look in the woods," Cee Cee said. "I can't go to town until I find her."

"That's silly."

"Well, I certainly don't want to go to town until I've looked. Let's check out the stone bridge and a couple of other places and then we'll go. Okay?"

"All right." Angel called out to her father and stepmother, "I'm going into the village with a friend." She grabbed her parka and car keys and she and Cee Cee started out the door.

"I'm not really grounded," Angel said.

Once they were on the porch, Angel tried to talk Cee Cee out of looking in the woods, but Cee Cee wheedled. "If we just give it a shot, then I can at least say I tried."

So they crossed into the birch forest and Cee Cee shouted into the distant woods for Jessica for about five minutes. Angel stood around looking both impatient and smug as Cee Cee led her farther and farther into the woods. When they reached the stone bridge, Cee Cee lunged and grabbed Angel's arm, twisting it tightly behind her back. "Now where is she?"

"Let me go."

Cee Cee jerked her arm and Angel screamed. "No one can hear you," Cee Cee said. "Tell me what you did!"

"I sent her a note to go to the tower. I signed it with Davey's name," Angel gasped.

"When?"

"A long time ago. My daddy is going to sue you if you hurt me. Let me go."

"You'll have to take me to the tower," Cee Cee demanded. "I don't know where it is."

"Let me go and I will."

Cee Cee let her go slightly and the minute she did so, she knew it was a mistake. Angel pushed her and ran off the little bridge.

Cee Cee lunged and grabbed for her. She caught her easily and pulled her arm back again. "You should get more exercise," Cee Cee said.

Angel was panting and red in the face, and Cee Cee was barely winded. But somehow, when Angel jerked away again, her sleeve ripped apart at the shoulder and Cee Cee lost her balance and tumbled into a pool of water. She came down with a crashing sound with Angel on top of her. She could feel the thud in every bone in her body as she hit the frozen ground.

There was a moment of darkness and then

there was a lot of pain. "We've got to get out of here," Cee Cee said.

"Let me go," Angel demanded.

Through the fog of pain, Cee Cee realized that her ankle was broken and she wouldn't be able to walk on it. Angel was pulling away but Cee Cee held on tight and said, "Let me think."

"Just let me go," Angel demanded. "I'm getting wet."

It was true. They were both lying in about four inches of icy water. The water would seep into their clothes and then they would really be miserable. Cee Cee thought a little farther. If she let Angel go, she would run away, and Cee Cee would still be lying in the water. I could die, Cee Cee thought. It was an amazing thought — one that made her a little ashamed of her foolishness.

"This is serious," Cee Cee said. "You'll have to help me up."

Angel cried, "I'm scared."

"Move off me and then pull me out of the water," Cee Cee commanded.

Instead of arguing, Angel rolled over onto the muddy bank, got up on her knees, and began to drag Cee Cee up out of the water. Cee Cee ground her teeth together to keep from screaming and held on tight to Angel's jacket. Soon, they were out of the water but Cee Cee could already feel her wet socks and pants turning to ice.

Angel insisted, "I have to go back and get cleaned up."

"I'm hurt," Cee Cee said through gritted teeth.

"Then let me go and I'll get help," Angel said quickly.

But she won't, Cee Cee thought. She'll just run off and leave me here.

As though she were reading her mind, Angel whined, "I'll send someone right back for you."

"Right," Cee Cee said. "You can't get up unless I figure out someway to get you to help me up." She continued to hold onto Angel and tried to sit up. Angel actually tried to help support her but it was hopeless. She couldn't sit up and she couldn't walk. "You'll have to carry me," Cee Cee said.

"I can't," Angel wailed. "I'm not strong at all."

They weren't too far into the woods, but Cee Cee was afraid Angel really wouldn't be able to do it. She said, "I'll hop and you hold me up. Help me up."

They struggled to get her to her feet but it was impossible. A couple of times, Cee Cee was quite sure that Angel was trying to get out of her grasp but she held on tight. She was still holding onto Angel's sleeve but she moved her grasp down a bit so she could get hold of her wrist as well.

"That hurts," Angel complained.

She held onto Angel and said, "Now, help me. This is not a joke. We've got to get help."

Angel said, "It's all your fault. If you hadn't made me do this, nothing would have happened."

Cee Cee said, "This is serious. If I let you go, will you go to the lodge and get help? Do you promise?"

Angel tried to move away from her, and Cee Cee jerked her hard, pulling her down beside her once again. She said, "Angel, if you run off, I could die. It is very important. You have to go back and you have to tell the truth."

Angel said, "It's all your fault."

Cee Cee nodded and said, "Let's not talk about fault. Let's talk about help. I can't walk. Do you promise?"

Angel tried to jerk away, and Cee Cee tightened her grip on Angel's arm. "Promise!"

Angel looked startled and said, "What good will it do? You won't be able to trust me anyway."

Cee Cee was sweating from the pain now

and she knew she might be going into shock. If Angel wouldn't help her voluntarily, she would have to outsmart her somehow. She said, "Now listen to me, Angel. Your father is a rich man and he loves his money. If you leave me out here and don't get help and I *do* get back, I'll sue you for millions and millions of dollars."

"I'll get help," Angel promised. She looked quite frightened now. "Only let me go. I'm scared."

"Millions and millions, Angel. And Jessica's father is a lawyer and so is Tonya's so I don't have to worry about legal fees."

"I promise," Angel said. "Now let me go."

Cee Cee let her go and slumped down on the ground. She wouldn't have been able to hold onto her much longer anyway. She was too tired and too weak and in too much pain.

Angel darted away as though she were a deer running from a hunter and Cee Cee wondered what would happen next. Whatever it is, Cee Cee thought, I'll just have to deal with it.

Cee Cee wished she'd worn a hat even though she didn't feel very cold. Was that a good or bad sign? She wasn't sure. She heard the wind begin to blow and felt clumps of ice from the birch trees pelt her. She curled up into a ball of pain, and tried to think of something pleasant. When that was absolutely impossible, she recited her multiplication tables aloud.

Chapter 35

Jessica and Davey were in the lodge hallway when Angel ran through the door. They faced her with angry looks.

"I need to talk to you," Davey said. He had just learned that Jessica waited in the cold tower for three hours while he was in town, and he knew there was only one person who could have possibly sent her that note.

"Call the ski patrol. Cee Cee's in the woods," Angel said. "She broke her ankle."

They were both so angry and ready to fight that it really didn't register for a moment. "What are you talking about?" Jessica asked.

"Cee Cee broke her ankle. She's at the stone bridge," Angel said. "You'd better go get her."

Jessica shook her head and said, "Angel, why would we believe you? You never tell the truth about anything."

"You've got to believe me about this," Angel said. "I promised."

Jessica shook her head again and started to walk away. Angel grabbed Davey's arm and said, "I know I haven't always told the truth but believe me on this. If I don't get help, Cee Cee said she's going to sue my father."

Davey said quietly to Jessica, "She's probably lying but there's just an off chance that she's telling the truth. She seems pretty upset."

Jessica nodded and they flew into action. Davey went immediately to the desk and asked for the ski patrol and the paramedics. Then he and Jessica went running out to the stone bridge.

When they got there, Cee Cee said, "I really did it this time." Then she passed out.

"Do we slap her face or what?" Jessica asked.

Davey bent over Cee Cee and listened to her breathing and said, "We'll wait. Help will be here in a minute."

The ski patrol was there first and carried her out on a stretcher as though she were as light as a doll. Jessica and Davey had a hard time keeping up with them, they moved so fast.

The ambulance was waiting and Jessica

laughed aloud when she saw that the paramedic was the red-haired man that Cee Cee had been looking for all week.

He looked quite cranky about being called out in the cold, and Jessica was afraid that behind his cross looks he was worried about Cee Cee's condition. But he said, "She's all right." That made Jessica feel better.

Jessica rode in the ambulance with Cee Cee. Davey went back to the lodge, saying he would borrow Madeline's car and bring the others along.

Cee Cee missed the ambulance ride entirely but the paramedic didn't seem worried about her. "She's passed out to avoid the pain," he said. "Normal reaction."

Even after they were in the hospital and Cee Cee woke up, Jessica was pretty sure she didn't recognize the paramedic who turned out to be a doctor.

He gave her a shot for pain and x-rayed the break. Then he set it himself, saying, "It's a simple fracture and will heal quickly. So I can save her a trip down to the Manchester Hospital."

"She's all right then?" Lauren asked.

"She's fine," he answered as he wrapped the ankle cast tightly up to her knee. "Clean break. She can go home if she wants."

"I don't think so," Tonya said. "I think she'd better stay here tonight. And you'll be here tomorrow, right?"

He smiled ruefully. "If she stays, I have to stay. This is a one-man hospital, at least tonight. My nurse's daughter is getting married tomorrow."

"She'd better stay," Lauren decided. "If you want, I'll stay with her." Then she seemed to rethink that and said, "Or Jessica can stay."

"I'll stay," he said. "It's my job. You kids go on back up to the lodge and have fun."

On the steps of the hospital, Lauren said, "I hope she's really all right. She sure seemed out of it."

Tonya burst out laughing and said, "She wasn't so out of it. When he said she could go home, she frowned at me and when I said she should stay, she winked."

"Oh well, that's all right," Lauren said. "That's more like Cee Cee."

Chapter 36

Jon was waiting for them in the lobby when they came in and he was obviously very pleased to hear that Cee Cee was all right. "The ski patrol guys weren't so sure."

Then he asked Tonya if she would take a walk with him. "I'm sorry about the night skiing," she said. "Too late now, I guess?"

"Yes. The lights go off at eleven, and it's almost ten-thirty," Jon said. "But I'd just as soon talk anyway." He brushed off a light dusting of snow on one of the porch swings and said, "Sit here with me, Tonya."

She sat as close to him as she dared. He reached over, took her hand, and said, "I was imagining how I would feel if I'd heard you were the girl on that stretcher. I would have been sick. So we ought to get some things straightened out. Right now."

"Right now?" She laughed and said, "No talk

about moonlight or roses. Just like that, huh?"

"First, I'm sorry I kissed you."

"I'm not."

"I'll never kiss you again without permission," he promised.

"You have my permission."

"And I want to talk about our future. You know, I'm a very serious guy."

"Kiss me, Jon." She turned and slipped her arms around his neck, pulling him close to her. He seemed startled, but pleased as he bent to kiss her lightly on the lips. Then he pulled away and said, "I can come and visit you in Danbury on my days off. Cee Cee says it's only four hours from here."

"Cee Cee talks too much," she said and buried her head in his shoulder. "Jon, I've got to tell you something. My dad got a big job in the new president's cabinet. We're moving to Washington, D.C., next week. The girls don't know it yet."

"That's all right," Jon said. "I have an uncle who's a professor at Howard University. I'll visit him a lot. In fact, I'll visit him all summer. Maybe take some summer courses. He'd like that."

"But aren't you going to New Zealand?" Her heart was thumping as she asked him. If Jon really liked her, and she knew now that he did, she wouldn't want to stand in the way of his career. On the other hand, New Zealand was halfway around the world.

"I'm taking a job at Mammoth next year. My coach is moving there and he got me a job, too. I was going to tell you that first thing but with all the excitement . . ." He stopped talking for a moment and kissed her again.

As she responded to his kiss, Tonya wondered if she would ever get used to the feelings between them. "Sparks," she murmured but Jon was talking again.

"The job starts in October and goes till June. You can visit me in California on vacations and I'll save up my days off and visit you in between."

She snuggled closer to him. Then she said, "Funny. I feel like I know you so well but there's a lot I don't know about you, Jon. You're full of surprises."

"You know the important things," he said. He bent to kiss her again and then put his arm around her and pointed up at the sky. "Moon's got a ring around it. Would you like that ring?"

Tonya laughed. "I don't think my parents are ready for me to come home from this trip with a ring. I'm supposed to be the sensible one. I'm only a junior in high school," she reminded him. But in her mind, she'd already decided to finish school this June and find a college. Maybe one in northern California next fall.

"Okay," Jon said easily. "Just as long as you and I know we're serious."

"Oh, Jon," Tonya teased as she drew his head down closer to hers so she could kiss him again, "that was the first thing I knew about you."

"Well I knew you were serious, too," Jon answered her companionably. "Otherwise, I wouldn't have bothered with you. I need a woman who can be solid and sensible. I couldn't stand a woman who couldn't make up her mind."

"Not to worry," Tonya promised him. "My mind is definitely made up."

Chapter 37

Cee Cee woke up and saw the tall young red-haired man standing at the foot of her bed. For one brief moment, she thought she was dreaming and then she asked, "Where have you been?"

He smiled and said, "I've been right here, Cee Cee. You're in the Paradise Medical Center and my name is Tucker O'Malley. People call me Dr. Tucker."

"But where have you been?" Cee Cee asked. "I looked for you all week."

"You haven't been sick for a week. You broke your ankle a few hours ago." He smiled and patted her arm and said, "I've given you some medicine that will make you groggy. You're friends thought you should spend the night here."

"Yes, I should," Cee Cee said. She was beginning to remember now. She'd been in the woods with Angel and . . . she frowned as she remembered the bad parts.

"Are you in pain?" Dr. Tucker asked. "You shouldn't be. You should be pretty sleepy tonight."

"How old are you?" she asked.

"I'm old enough to be a doctor," he laughed. "My degree's hanging on the wall in my office. I'll show it to you tomorrow morning."

"But how old are you?"

"Would you like some water? How about anything else. There's a chair there." He pointed to a wheelchair with a potty in it. Cee Cee shook her head quickly. This was obviously going to be difficult — how could she get him to see her as a girl instead of a patient?

"You don't look very old," she said. "Are you married?"

He laughed and shook his head. "I'm twenty-three. I just got out of medical school and this is my first internship. And I barely had time to talk to women in the last six years, let alone get married."

"I'm nineteen," Cee Cee volunteered.

"You're sixteen," he corrected and held up her chart. "And I've got two other patients down the hall so I'll see you in the morning."

"But can I ring the bell if I need you?"

"Sure," Dr. Tucker said. "I'm on twenty-four hour call."

"You sleep here?"

He nodded and said, "Now get some sleep. It's midnight."

"Why did you wake me?" she asked.

"To give you a sleeping pill," he answered.

"Is that a joke?"

He looked so startled at the suggestion that she smiled and asked, "You don't have much of a sense of humor, do you?"

"I'm a doctor," he answered. "Not a comedian."

"But laughter is the latest thing in medicine. I'll have to teach you how to laugh." Cee Cee felt herself beginning to drift off and she recognized that it must be the medicine that he'd given her. Never mind, she'd found the key to romance with Dr. Tucker.

Chapter 38

Thursday

They called the hospital first thing in the morning and found out from Dr. Tucker that "Cee Cee had a good night" and was still sleeping. He said they could pick her up anytime between eleven and two.

"We'd better make it two," Tonya said. "By that time the bubble will have burst and she'll be ready to come back to the lodge."

"Not everyone's bubble bursts," Lauren protested. "Yours didn't. You told us yourself you're engaged."

"Not engaged," Tonya smiled.

"But it sounded pretty serious to me," Jessica said. She was trying not to think about the phone call she would make in a few hours. Her mother said the Boston lab promised to have the results by ten-thirty. That was only three hours away. I've waited this long, Jessica told herself, I can wait a little longer.

"You and Davey looked pretty serious your-selves," Tonya said.

Jessica smiled. "Funny, Cee Cee was so sure she'd have such a great romantic *week*. You found Jon, Tonya, and I found . . . I found Davey, but . . ." Her voice broke and Tonya looked at her sharply.

"This is our last skiing day," Lauren said. "Let's ski." She stood up as Marshall came over to the table with a pot of coffee in his hand.

He had a beige envelope in his other hand, and Jessica worried that doing two things at once would confuse him. It was a good thing Marshall was an excellent student; he would never make a career as a waiter.

Jessica ducked automatically and Lauren laughed. "I'm in such a good mood, I'm even glad to see Marshall," she admitted. When the tall, awkward boy came closer, Lauren said, "Hi, Marshall. Cee Cee says you're interested in marine biology. Want to meet me after lunch and we can take a walk in the woods together. You can tell me all about it."

Marshall opened his mouth, squeaked, "Sure," and turned and practically ran back to the kitchen.

"Now you're in for it," Tonya warned. "He'll

follow you like a puppy dog the rest of the trip."

"It's only one day," Lauren answered, "and he's probably very nice when you get to know him. He's just a little shy."

She and Tonya struck out for Devil's Run together and Jessica said she'd stay on the intermediate slopes. There was a much bigger difference in their ability after they'd had full days of practice but Jessica didn't care. She'd had a much better time with Davey than she'd anticipated.

As Tonya and Lauren stood at the top of Devil's Run, Tonya asked, "How do you think Jessica is doing?"

Lauren looked a little surprised and said, "Jessica's different and I'm not sure why. I don't think it has anything to do with Davey so it must be that secret."

Tonya nodded. "I think we'd better talk to her soon."

"Yes," Lauren agreed. "We'll talk to her."

Jessica skied until ten and then went back to the lobby and called home. There was no answer so she tried again at ten-forty-five and again at eleven. She tried every fifteen minutes until noon and there was simply no answer.

By twelve-fifteen, she was really worried.

Where was everyone? Why weren't they answering the phone? As she waited between the phone rings, she felt her stomach knot up so tightly that she thought she might throw up. She was really frightened now. No news had to be bad news in this case. She imagined her mother sitting huddled by the phone, so upset that she couldn't even answer it.

But where was her dad? He should be hovering over her, and so he should be able to answer the telephone. Unless her mother was taking the news so hard that they'd taken her to the doctor. It isn't fair, Jessica thought. This is my problem, not hers.

"What are you doing?" Tonya's voice was over her shoulder.

"Where's Lauren?" Jessica asked. "I thought we were going to have lunch before we picked up Cee Cee?"

"She's breaking Marshall's heart," Tonya said. "She promised she'd take a walk with him but we have to pick up Cee Cee. You ready?"

"Give me a few minutes," Jessica said. "I want to change out of these ski clothes."

Tonya looked at her very curiously but nodded her head, saying, "I'll wait here."

Jessica went to her room and changed into her blue sweater and a pair of Levi's. It was warm outside and she felt like wearing something old and comfortable. I guess there are comfort clothes as well as comfort food, she thought. She smiled at herself in the mirror. The reflection that looked back at her wasn't smiling. What she saw in her blue eyes was pure fear. You're scared, Jessica, and it shows.

As she looked in the mirror, she felt herself get farther and farther away, as if she were distancing herself from the reflection in the mirror. She could feel sweat popping out on her forehead, her breathing was becoming short and shallow, and she was getting lightheaded and dizzy. She thought for a moment that she might faint.

Maybe this is what dying is like, she thought. Maybe it's just moving farther and farther away from life. The idea seemed to come from her stomach and life was very distant for a moment.

"Don't be silly," she said out loud and turned and forced herself to put on her regular jacket and meet her girlfriends.

She phoned once from the lobby before they left. "Nice of Angel's father to rent us the limo," Jessica said as she slipped into the backseat of the large white Cadillac that was waiting outside the lodge.

"He's just lucky no one is suing him," Tonya said.

"You know Cee Cee doesn't have a case," Jessica chided. "She's the one who forced Angel into that adventure in the first place."

"Speaking of Angel," Tonya said. "Has anyone seen her?"

"I think she really is grounded," Lauren offered. "Marshall said she's calling room service every hour or two."

"Roast pheasant," Tonya guessed.

"And champagne cocktails," Jessica giggled in spite of her fear.

"Caviar," Lauren added.

"Hard to think of Angel on bread and water, that's for sure," Tonya said.

"Davey says Angel has a terrible life," Jessica said.

"Sure she does," Tonya answered. "No one gets that weird without some sort of history. But things won't get any better for her unless something changes. I hope they do ground her for a while."

"And I hope Angel's father really meant it when he said we should have lunch wherever we wanted," Lauren added. They were pulling into a fancy restaurant which was on the highway not too far from the village. They'd heard about it but they'd never actually seen it.

Jessica called again before they were seated and after they ordered. Tonya said, "What's up? Why all the phone calls?"

"My folks aren't home," Jessica said.

"I thought they were going into New York City."

"They cancelled," Jessica said.

"Why?"

"Oh, I don't know. This salad dressing is marvelous."

"Jessica, it's time for us to have a little chat."

"What about?" Jessica crumbled her bread and put it down.

"We're worried about you . . . " Tonya began. Then she stopped and began again, "Maybe I can make it easier for you. I'll tell my secret first. When I came up here I knew I was moving next week but I didn't want to ruin everyone's trip. So I kept it a secret."

"Moving!" both Jessica and Lauren exclaimed.

"I can't believe it!" Lauren said.

"It's awful," Jessica cried.

Tonya was frightened by the stricken look on Jessica's face. "I hoped if I told you my secret, you'd tell yours."

Jessica put down her fork and shook her head. "Is this secret confession time? If it is, I'm not having anything to do with it."

Lauren said, "I'll tell my secret, too. Everyone probably guessed it anyway. But the truth is, I'm terrified of these guys up here. They're all too grown-up for me and they treat me different from the way they treat you and Cee Cee. I'm just a kid. I can't help it if I grew to be five feet eleven. Brian is the only guy I've ever really been comfortable with and I've cried myself to sleep nearly every night."

"You liked Greg," Tonya reminded her.

"Yes, I did like Greg, until I found out that I couldn't trust him, either," Lauren said.

Lauren and Tonya looked expectantly at Jessica. Tonya said, "You've got that runaway, faraway look in your eye, kiddo. We're not going to let you get away with it."

"I still don't know why or where you're moving," Jessica said.

"On January fourth my family and I are going to be in Washington, D.C. My father is going to be an economic advisor to the President and we've got to be there for the inauguration. Now it's your turn."

Jessica shook her head. If she told them now, their vacation would be ruined. And besides, she might start crying right here in the middle of this fancy restaurant.

"You can't get out of this, Jessica," Tonya said. "We know something bad is going on. I don't know what it is but I have a horrible feeling it has to do with your health. Whatever it is, honey, we want to share it with you. We're your friends."

Jessica swallowed, then gulped and nodded and her voice came out in a whisper as she told her story. "I thought it would just be a mistake. When I dropped that big platter before Christmas, they took X rays and they said I might have a brain tumor. Then I had to have some other tests and I've been waiting all week for the results. I guess I know what they are now."

"Brain tumor," Lauren said softly. She was obviously awed by the words.

"You got the results today?"

"Not really," Jessica said. "I was *supposed* to get them but my folks aren't home. I think my mom is probably in shock and had to go to the hospital or something."

"But maybe the results were good and they just went away," Tonya suggested.

"No," Jessica said. "They would stay by the phone and tell me. They know I've been worried half out of my mind. No — either my mom's really in bad shape or they can't bear to tell me till I get home."

"You can still hope. You don't really know yet, and brain tumors can be operated on,"

Tonya insisted. But what Jessica said made sense. The only other possibility she could think of was that Mr. and Mrs. Mitchell were driving up here right now to take Jessica home with them. She hoped that wasn't the case and she didn't suggest it to Jessica.

"Apparently not the one I have."

"Think you have," Lauren said softly.

"I was supposed to get the final results on Monday but the tests had to be further analyzed. So it's been a really hard week," Jessica said. "I do better if I focus on what's going on right now. Like this salad." She forked a quarter of a tomato and put it in her mouth but then she laid her fork down again and sighed. "It doesn't always work."

"I wish you'd told us," Lauren said.

"Why?" Jessica snapped. "You think it's easier for me if you all sit around and look miserable? You should see your faces."

"We're in shock," Tonya said briskly. Then she smiled slightly and asked, "So you've spent the whole trip waiting for the other shoe to drop? No wonder you haven't been more upset about Angel and Davey and all that nonsense."

Jessica nodded. "The funny part is that I really like Davey. But, of course, he doesn't know."

"Doesn't know you like him?" Tonya asked. "Or doesn't know you may be sick?"

"Both."

"You're wrong on both counts," Tonya said. "Anyone can tell you like him and Angel told Cee Cee she thinks you're sick so it's a cinch she told the same tale to Davey."

Jessica sighed and said, "You know something? I feel better now that I've told you, and maybe you're right. Maybe now is the time to tell Davey. Now, not later."

"Good girl," Tonya said. "Well, shall we go over and see if we can talk Cee Cee into coming home? I hope she's not so crazy about that red-haired intern that she refuses to leave."

Chapter 39

Cee Cee woke at seven that morning and rang the bell for Dr. Tucker. A nurse answered and Cee Cee asked, "Where is he?"

"Treating two children with frostbite," the nurse answered before she popped a thermometer into Cee Cee's mouth.

Cee Cee took the thermometer out of her mouth and said, "I'll wait for Dr. Tucker." Then she clamped her teeth shut and crossed her hands over her chest so that the nurse couldn't take her pulse. Instead of arguing with her, the nurse laughed and shook her head.

A few minutes later, Tucker O'Malley came in and took her blood pressure and temperature. As he put the thermometer in her mouth, he said, "This is special treatment, you know."

She took the thermometer out, "You promised you'd take care of me. Why did you call a nurse?"

He grinned. "Self-protection."

"Won't do you any good," she said.

"Maybe not," he answered, "but it seemed sensible under the circumstances. You been up here long?"

"Almost a week," she said. "We go home tomorrow."

"But you were here when I got here," he said.

"That was you! I saw you in the hallway that first afternoon. It was you, wasn't it?"

He nodded. "First day on the job. My folks and I had dinner at the lodge and toured the place. Met the ski patrol. The regular stuff."

They talked for a while and Cee Cee found out that this was his first independent residency. He was part of an outreach program of the hospital in Manchester. "They don't have enough demand for a real doctor," he said. "So they take interns like me and pay us for the paramedic part of the operation."

"So that's why you're so young," Cee Cee speculated. "You have more schooling to complete." That's good, she decided. When he really has time to fall in love, I'll be old enough.

"I'm going on to specialize in orthopedics," he said.

"Bones?"

"Bones. By the way, the hospital called your

parents and told them about your accident." He left then but came back every hour or so just to chat. Cee Cee decided that he was bored and lonely so each time he visited her, she asked him more questions about his work and his life.

About ten-thirty, he said, "You have two choices. Either I can send you home in a cab and save your friends a trip or you can help me entertain two sick kids down the hall. Nurse Wiggens went home and I've got some paperwork to do."

She looked up at him and grinned. "Are you kidding?"

"No, I'm not kidding," he said, quite seriously. "I could use the help. I don't know much about what to do with these kids, but they're not ready to go home yet."

"I'd love to help you."

He helped her into the wheelchair, and as he lifted her, his head bent close to hers and she turned slightly. His breath was on her cheek, and she felt a delicious thrill go down her neck and shoulders. She shivered, and he asked, "Cold?"

"No," she answered, "not cold. Not cold at all." She was trying very hard to act grown-up but she couldn't help being sixteen. Funny part was, he seemed to think she was perfectly all right just the way she was.

She thought he was the nicest young man she had ever met. They had the same red hair but that wasn't all they had in common. They both liked to read mysteries and they both liked Elvis Presley. For Cee Cee, that was enough to build a real future together.

Now as he pushed the wheelchair down the hall, he asked her, "Are you thinking of a career in medicine?"

"Definitely." She didn't add that she was actually more interested in a career as a doctor's wife.

Just before they got to the other room she asked, "Do you have a special girlfriend?"

He patted her on the shoulder and said, "Just you, Cee Cee, just you."

"That's fine," Cee Cee replied. "That's the right answer." They both laughed, and she could tell that instead of finding her forwardness unnerving, he thought she was very cute. She liked the idea of having a boyfriend she could be herself around. He probably thought he was safe because he was so much older but he'd see.

"There's not a lot of difference between sixteen and twenty-three, you know."

"Seven years," he said quickly. "That's a lot of difference, Cee Cee."

"But it won't be anything at all when you're twenty-seven and I'm twenty," she pointed out.

"These kids are kind of bored, and scared. You'll be just what the doctor ordered."

"I'm almost seventeen. It could be a long courtship."

"Seven-year courtships are unlucky," he answered quickly and wheeled her into the room where the two kids were. "Hi, kids. Here's Cee Cee. She believes in the therapeutic value of laughter so I brought her to see you."

Cee Cee said hello to the twins and asked, "Which of you is Zack?"

"I am," they both said in unison.

"Okay," Cee Cee said. "I'll call you Zack Left and Zack Right. How's that?"

Zack Left said, "I remember you — you're the funny girl." Then he laughed.

His brother said, "You kept falling down."

Cee Cee blushed. She didn't want Dr. Tucker to know what a fool she had made of herself over the lift operator, but she was glad that the kids were so obviously glad to see her.

"Dr. Tucker has to do some paperwork. So let's do something fun."

"There's no TV," Zack Left complained.

"We'll tell jokes," Cee Cee offered. "I'll go first. Do you know when a singer isn't a singer?"

The boys shook their heads back and forth.

"When he's a little hoarse!" Cee Cee said.

Neither boy laughed, but Dr. Tucker laughed and laughed. Then he said, "I see the situation's under control. I'll be back soon."

"Don't you know any jokes?" Cee Cee asked.

Dr. Tucker smiled and patted Cee Cee on the head and said, "If you have trouble, ring. I'm going to grab a bite to eat and finish my charts."

Cee Cee flashed him her most charming smile and said, "Don't forget me."

She spent a good hour with the twins and then their mother came for them. As she and Tucker watched the two boys leave with their mom, she said, "So when I leave, you'll be all alone? Do they let you go out?"

"With my beeper," he answered.

"How about with a girl?"

He laughed and said, "Cee Cee, I think you're too sophisticated for me."

"I know you think seven years is a lot but in the eye of eternity, it's nothing."

"How do you think your folks would like

hearing us explain about the eye of eternity?" he asked.

He does like me, Cee Cee decided. She ignored his question about her parents and said, "I was just going to ask if you wanted to come to the lodge tonight. Big New Year's Eve party and a disc jockey and free food and pretty girls. Look, I know you think I'm just a kid and all, but what are you doing New Year's Eve?"

He laughed. "What could I be doing? I don't know a soul up here except you."

"People won't be falling down and breaking their necks until really late in the evening," Cee Cee predicted. "And I'm sure they can find you with your beeper."

"What's all this leading up to, Cee Cee?"

"I'm inviting you to be my date for New Year's Eve."

Tucker smiled and asked, "You mean come to the lodge and go to a party with you, right?"

"Oh yeah, perfectly harmless. You'll be safe with me."

His nose crinkled when he laughed, Cee Cee noticed. "So you'll come?" she persisted.

"Sure," Tucker answered. "I'd love to join your party. But I'm too old to be your date."

"So you said," Cee Cee said triumphantly.

"What time shall I arrive? And what should I wear?"

"Do you have a tuxedo?"

"No, but I do have a dark blue suit," he answered.

Cee Cee decided she would definitely pull the box of dressy clothes from under the bed. Despite her friend's objections, she had called the first day and asked her mother to send dress-up clothes by UPS.

Cee Cee said confidently, "I don't know how I'll look with this pink cast on my leg, but I am definitely dressing up." Then she quickly added, "I'm so glad to have a real live date for New Year's Eve, with a real live doctor."

"This is not really a date," he cautioned.

"You should smile more," Cee Cee said. "You look a lot better when you smile."

He laughed. "It will be fun for me to talk to someone. I'll see you at about seven tonight. All right?"

"In the tux?"

"In the blue suit," Tucker promised her.

I'll have to break him to my mother gently, Cee Cee decided. First, I'll tell her about this nice doctor and she'll imagine he's about sixty-five and then I'll say he just happens to be passing through town and can I have dinner with him. When she sees him, she'll know he's not sixty-five and that's when I'll tell her about the eye of eternity.

When her friends came to pick her up, Tonya asked, "What did you do to that guy? He seemed so serious last night and now he seems really cheerful."

"Maybe he's glad to get rid of me," Cee Cee said demurely and then she laughed aloud. "Have I got a surprise for you guys! I've got a date with Prince Charming, after all."

Chapter 40

After they brought Cee Cee home, they told her about Tonya's and Jessica's secrets. For once, she had nothing very funny to say. She hugged Jessica and said, "Whatever happens, I'll be there."

Jessica hugged her back and stood up, saying, "I'm going to find Davey now. I've got to tell him."

"Try your house again," Tonya said. "Don't give up hope."

"I will," Jessica promised, "but I'm certain now that they're waiting till I get home tomorrow to break the bad news. I know they're trying to help me, but I wish . . ." Her voice broke and she grabbed her ski parka and left the room.

She tried one more time to call home and when she got no response, she decided to look for Davey. He was supposed to be helping with the decorations for the New Year's Eve party so she went to the lounge first but the room was strewn with crepe paper and paper lanterns and was obviously already decorated. Davey wasn't there.

When she passed the phones in the lobby, she sighed and tried again. Then she climbed the stairs to the second floor. Maybe Davey was in the library.

He was playing her song on the guitar and he looked up and smiled when she entered the room. "I really like this, Jessica. I think it's good enough to publish. Mind if I check it out with a few of my Hollywood friends?"

"Sure, go ahead," Jessica answered. "I need to talk to you."

He looked sharply at her and asked, "How are you doing?"

She answered, "Not very well. I need to explain to you that I've known something all week that I haven't shared with anyone. I just told the girls and I want to tell you."

She told him her story quickly, leaving nothing out, including the terror she'd felt as she went through the suspense of waiting. "So now, I guess the suspense is over," she finished. "They would be answering the phone if the news were good."

Davey's face betrayed how upset he was,

and he took her hands and said, "Don't give up, Jessica. Never give up. Let's expect the best together."

Jessica nodded her head and said, "Sure. But I needed to tell you so you could be prepared for the worst. Davey, I don't plan to see you again after tonight."

"Why not?" Now he looked even more upset.

"It's not fair to you," Jessica answered slowly. "It's different with my parents and the girls. They pretty much will have to hang in there. But you're different. You can let go right now and I've decided you should."

"It doesn't make any difference," he said. Davey leaned over and kissed her cheek. "I love you, Jessica. I love everything about you. Why do you think I'd stop loving you if it turns out you have something wrong, physically?"

"This isn't something wrong physically," Jessica said as she brushed tears from her cheeks. "This is a brain tumor that kills people. Six months, more or less. I looked it up."

"Six months is a lifetime if you're in love," Davey said.

Jessica jumped up and said, "You don't know what you're talking about! We just met and we're not in love. Now, let me alone!"

Davey stood up beside her and hugged her,

then kissed her cheek again. "Hold on, Jessica. It's me — Davey. We're friends, remember? You don't need to yell at me to get rid of me. It won't work, you know."

She began to sob then, really letting the heartbreaking, deep sobs well up and burst from her chest. As she cried, Davey held her and smoothed her back and whispered in her ear, "Poor Jessica, you've had a really hard time, haven't you? Poor, poor Jessica. I do love you, you know."

Eventually, she was through crying and she said, "I'm all right now."

"Let's go for a walk," Davey suggested. "See what the great outdoors can do to cheer us up."

They took each other's hands and walked down the stairs and through the hallway and lobby out onto the clearing in front of the woods. "Let's go see our bridge," Davey said.

"I think it's Cee Cee's bridge now. Guess what? She actually talked that grumpy young doctor into coming to the party tonight."

"Cee Cee can be very persuasive," Davey said.

When they finally got to the little bridge they stopped and Davey said, "This is where I kissed you the first time. Remember?"

"But I kissed you first," Jessica reminded him.

"Ah, but you kissed me to spite Angel," Davey teased. "I kissed you out of love."

"Poor Angel," Jessica said. "I wonder what will become of her."

"She'll marry money and live unhappily ever after," Davey predicted.

"At least she'll marry and have kids," Jessica said softly.

Davey dropped his arm around her shoulder and asked, "You didn't tell me because you were afraid I would dump you, right?"

"Not really," Jessica said. "It was more just that I wanted to handle it myself. But Tonya and Lauren convinced me that it's better to share with people who care about you, no matter how it turns out."

"I better thank Tonya and Lauren, because I guessed something was wrong at the very beginning, and I was thinking that you really didn't like me very much."

"Oh Davey, I like you better than any boy I've ever met."

With that, he put his arms around her and kissed her and she felt a soft, silent, sweet closeness that seemed as though it would last forever. They stood on the bridge for a long time, silently holding each other's hands, looking down at the icy water.

Finally, Davey said, "Whatever happens, you mean a lot to me and I want to go through it with you, whatever it is. You're my girl, Jessie, and nobody, no thing, is going to stop that." He put his arm around her and hugged her close to him.

She leaned her head onto his shoulder and said, "Davey, I want you for my boyfriend. I want us to have a long, wonderful future together . . . but . . ."

"No buts," he said. Then he added, "I had something else to ask you, Jessica. I was thinking maybe I could talk you into going to an eastern music school. Maybe Juilliard or Eastman or even Oberlin. How about that?"

"I don't think I'm good enough," Jessica answered.

"You're better than you know," Davey said. "Anyway, I think I'll choose a music school on the East Coast. It will be a compromise for my mom and dad and their eternal battles and it will bring me closer to you."

'Davey . . ."

He held up his hand and touched her lips lightly. "Let me have my dream, Jessica. Let the dream last as long as it can."

"All right," she agreed. "I'll think about

schools and talk it over with my folks when we get home. It's a year away for me but it's about time I started thinking about them anyway." If Davey wanted to play this game, she would play it with him. After all, she was an expert.

Davey held her close and had the good sense to say nothing else. After a while he kissed her again. He kissed both her eyes and her forehead, her nose and her cheeks. Then he kissed her on the lips and said, "We'd better go in. I'm kind of glad we don't have to perform tonight. We can have a real date. But the boss's wife asked me if you'd be coming back soon. You're really a hit. Too bad you have to go back and finish high school."

Jessica laced her fingers in Davey's and they turned and walked back toward the lodge. Even though her heart was bursting with sadness, she was very happy. It was a little like having sunshine while it rained.

Chapter 41

"You're coming to the party tonight," Tonya said. "That's definite."

"Do I really have to?" Jon asked. "Couldn't we just go somewhere quiet and watch TV?"

"You're coming," Tonya said. "Cee Cee has a date with her doctor. Jessica and Davey will be there and they don't have to perform. And Lauren has asked Marshall."

"I guess if Marshall can handle it, I can," Jon said. "I don't own a jacket."

"Wear a sweater then. You do have real shoes?"

"Sort of." Jon looked doubtful and then he asked, "Are loafers real?"

"Yes." Tonya laughed and bent over and picked up some of the clean snow they were standing on. She skied off from the hill, then turned and threw a snowball at Jon. "Can't catch me," she called.

"I'll give you a head start and still catch you," he called.

"Never," Tonya called back. She was going pretty fast and she thought she might be able to beat him.

Jon skied right after her and caught up with her about three-quarters of the way down the mountain. When he caught her, they both fell over and they were soon rolling around in the snow.

Tonya pretended to try and get away from him as they wrestled in the snow but she knew she would never let him go if she could help it. Jon pinned her down and kissed her. She stopped fighting and circled his shoulders with her arms, drawing him closer.

Jon's warm breath on her cheek and on her neck stirred the now familiar electricity within her and she felt a heat rising within that she had never felt before. She was flushed with warmth and excitement and she was enjoying every minute of it.

Once in a while, she pretended to try and get away from him but he held her tight. She laughed and said, "No, Jon, let me go," knowing her laughter was an invitation to continue.

She enjoyed teasing Jon, and she enjoyed being pursued by him.

Can this be me? she asked herself. It seemed almost as though she was standing outside, watching herself play this game. She was really surprised she could let her guard down like this. And she was amazed how much she enjoyed flirting with Jon.

Then Jon pulled her closer and kissed her deeply. She wound her arms around his neck and they were lying in a full embrace on the snow. "Tonya," Jon said in a deep, sexy voice, "let's skip the party tonight. You can come to my room instead."

"I don't know," Tonya said. She wasn't frightened at his suggestion but she wasn't sure she wanted to follow through on it, either. This was all so new to her and she had a feeling that she was discovering what the words "playing with fire" really meant.

About then, Lauren came whizzing down the mountain, and she stopped next to them, calling out, "Are you hurt?"

Jon pulled Tonya to her feet and they both grinned foolishly. Lauren still didn't seem to understand what she'd broken up and she kept asking, "Did you fall? Are you hurt?"

"She's in good shape," Jon assured her

gravely. "But you'd better take her back to the lodge before she gets into trouble."

As Tonya skied away from Jon, she turned and laughed. He laughed, too, and called to her, "I'll see you at the party."

Chapter 42

Cee Cee was so pleased with herself when she dragged the big box of dresses out from under the bed that none of the others chided her for her foolishness. "Everything came from my closet," she announced proudly.

The other three girls looked at the dresses and then burst into laughter. "What do you think I'm going to wear?" Tonya asked.

"I thought the yellow-striped taffeta with the purple trim," Cee Cee said.

"Not in this lifetime," Tonya said grimly.

"I'll try it," Jessica offered, though she was very glad when the sleeves were too tight.

Lauren did agree to wear the lime-green knit skirt, black sweater, and Cee Cee's rhinestone earrings. The skirt was so short and tight on Lauren that it looked quite stylish with her black stockings and low flat shoes.

"You can have my red dress," Cee Cee said

to Jessica. "I had Mom put in this navy taffeta for you, but I can't wear the red one with my pink cast."

"Because it clashes?" Jessica didn't think Cee Cee ever thought about things like that.

"No, because the skirt is too long and tight for the cast. The navy taffeta is full." Cee Cee made a face. "I've had it since eighth grade but at least it's shiny and has a low neckline."

So Jessica wore Cee Cee's bright red dress and only Tonya stuck to her guns and wore her best slacks and sweater. "You look great," Cee Cee admitted, "but I still think you should try on the yellow satin."

"Nope. Jon wouldn't like it," Tonya said. It was easier to blame it on Jon than to tell the truth. As far as Tonya was concerned, Cee Cee had impossible taste in clothes.

"It is fun to be dressed up," Jessica said to Tonya as they walked down the hallway to the party. Lauren was wheeling Cee Cee along behind them. "At least she was thinking of us."

"She'll never know how lucky she is that she couldn't get into anything but that navy-blue dress," Tonya said. "She looks nice."

As they stood in the lobby waiting for Jon and Tucker, Cee Cee said, "Okay, this is the evening of my life. I've got the dream date that I've always wanted, and I'm going to have a wonderful time. Look, there's Dr. Tucker. Isn't he gorgeous?"

Then Tonya spotted Jon. He looked wonderful in his gray sweater and gray slacks, and white shirt and red tie. He kissed her hello and said, "You look beautiful."

She smiled and tucked her arm in his and said, "I could eat a horse."

Jon said, "No horses are served here, but how about a nice fat little chicken?"

"Okay," Tonya replied and they went on into the dining room to snag a good table.

Angel was there with her stepmother and father and Tonya stopped long enough to say, "Thanks for the limousine and the lunch. Cee Cee is fine."

"That's good," Angel's father said. Angel didn't even look up.

"So much for making amends with Little Miss Angel," Tonya muttered, but Angel's father sent a bottle of champagne to their table later.

When the champagne arrived, Tucker said to Cee Cee, "You can't drink that."

"I know," Cee Cee said. She held up her water glass and said, "I'd like to propose a toast."

Jon said, "Wait a minute and I'll get some ginger ale for the youngsters."

"Who do you think you are?" Tonya asked.

In the end, only Tucker had champagne and the rest of them drank ginger ale as Cee Cee toasted, "To the future."

Davey looked deep into Jessica's eyes and clinked the rim of his glass on hers. "To the future," he said.

"To the future," she agreed and smiled at him.

After dinner, they all went into the lounge where Davey proudly showed off his handiwork, pointing out that he had had to climb high on a ladder to attach the crepe paper streamers.

Tucker seemed to have a good time with Cee Cee and he talked a lot to Jon about skiing as well. Marshall didn't say much of anything but he managed to get through dinner without spilling soup on anyone so Tonya figured the evening was going to be a success.

When Tucker saw Lauren, Cee Cee was worried that she would lose him, but he obviously remembered all her friends from the night before and didn't seem particularly impressed by Lauren's beauty. Doctors probably believe that stuff about beauty being skin-deep, Cee Cee decided. Nevertheless, she was glad when Lauren started dancing with every man who asked her. It made it easier to keep Tucker's attention on her.

She knew he thought she was just a nice, funny kid, but Cee Cee was confident that she had a good chance to help him see better during the next seven years. And he was an absolutely marvelous date for a girl with a cast. He wheeled Cee Cee over to help the disc jockey pick out records, and he refilled her drink whenever it was empty. He asked her questions about school and herself. He pretended to be surprised when she said she was a cheerleader, and they had a lot of fun.

Angel stopped by about ten and said, "Hi, I just thought I'd come over and let you thank me for saving your life."

"Yeah, right," Cee Cee said, knowing full well that Angel had dropped by to see her date. "Angel, this is Dr. Tucker.

"Dr. Tucker, this is the girl who broke my ankle or saved my life, depending on which version you like."

Angel smiled and batted her eyelashes. "I thought maybe you were Cee Cee's older brother. You have the same color hair."

"No, we have the same barber," Tucker answered.

Cee Cee stared at him. It was the first time she'd heard him try to be funny.

Angel put her hand on his arm and asked,

"Would you like to dance with me? I know Cee Cee is out of commission, but I don't have a date tonight."

Tucker shook his head. "No, Cee Cee and I agreed to sit the whole evening out. Sorry."

About that time someone came up and asked Angel to dance, and she drifted away in a cloud of sweet, light perfume.

"Not your favorite friend? Is she?"

"No, she's not," Cee Cee said. "But she did probably save my life, so I probably would have let her dance with you if I had to."

Tucker leaned closer and whispered, "I don't know how to dance."

Cee Cee nodded. "Too much work and no play. I'll teach you."

He looked surprised but didn't object to the idea. "I worked all through high school and premed. I just never learned."

"You're lucky you met me."

"I have medical loans to pay off for the next twenty years," he said. "Fun isn't real high on my list of priorities."

Cee Cee nodded. "Sometimes priorities change when you meet the right person." Then she added confidently, "I'm a lot of fun, you know."

Tucker smiled. "You are that. You're a great kid, Cee Cee."

Cee Cee smiled back. She had many plans for the next few years, and one of her plans was to convince him that she was no kid. But she didn't want to rush him. "Tell me how you worked in high school. Was that hard?"

When his beeper went off at eleven o'clock, she had a good idea he'd staged it in advance but she didn't really mind. She *was* kind of tired and she had time on her side. "Wheel me to my room?" Cee Cee asked.

"I can't," he said. "I have to get back to the hospital."

"I'll take you to your room," Lauren offered.

Cee Cee knew when she was beat. She raised her hands and drew Dr. Tucker down to her level, then kissed him full on the lips. "Happy New Year," she said. "We'll be in touch."

He looked a little surprised and then he laughed. "I had a good time, Cee Cee. Thanks for inviting me."

She nodded her head. Time was on her side.

Chapter 43

Tonya and Jon danced together the whole evening. At about a quarter of twelve Jon turned to her and said, "This has been the most wonderful week of my life, Tonya. I hate to let you go. Even for a little while."

"It's been wonderful for me, too." Tonya nestled her head against his shoulder and sighed. "I'll see you in Washington in the spring."

"Cherry blossom time," Jon promised. "I'll get some kind of work down there for the summer. Will your folks mind?"

"I don't think so," Tonya said slowly. They would be surprised, she was certain of that, but they would like Jon when they got to know him.

The music stopped but Jon slipped both arms around her waist and drew her closer to him. "I just want to know that you're going to be there when I come back in April. I want to know that while I'm building my skiing career that my home base can be Washington, D.C. I want to be able to count on you. I want to be able to count on the future."

"Oh Jon," she sighed. "How can any of us know what the future will bring?" She was thinking now of Jessica and how unstable her life was, and how you just really couldn't count on anything. "We just can't plan that far in advance."

"I can," Jon said with definite determination. "I plan on going to Mammoth and winning prizes. Then I'll get on the racing circuit for a few years and make some money. Then I'll be teaching skiing once again. I'm hoping to make the U.S. Olympic team, and I'm planning to make a whole lot of money on commercials. Did you know that some of my friends who have been around a little longer are making a hundred or two hundred thousand dollars a year endorsing Chap Stick? You're dancing with a rich man, Tonya."

She laughed and said, "Do you think I fell in love with you for your money?"

"And I plan on putting that money in the bank. You're good with money. You can invest it. By the time you've finished two years of college, we'll be wealthy homeowners, married, and talking about starting a family."

Tonya laughed and said, "You paint such pretty pictures."

"And the house will have vines growing all around it, and roses in the front yard, and a picket fence," Jon said. "Can I count on you?" He looked deep into her eyes.

She looked up at him and saw that he wasn't kidding. He wanted an answer, and the answer would be a commitment. "I don't know," Tonya said. "I don't know if I'm ready for that kind of commitment."

Jon's grip tightened around her waist. He leaned over and kissed her on the cheek and kissed behind her ear. He nuzzled into her neck and lightly bit her earlobe and said, "You're ready, Tonya. We're both ready for commitment. We're both very grown-up and we both know exactly what we want. And what I want is you." Then the New Year's Eve whistles went off and he kissed her. Tonya let herself melt in his arms and time seemed to slip away. In that moment, there was no one else in her world except Jon. Jon was solid, he was stable, and he was her friend.

When they finally let go of each other, he said, "Happy New Year."

She said, "Happy New Year, Jon. Yes, I'll be expecting you in April."

"That's a start," Jon said. "We'll work on planting the roses along about June when you graduate from high school and I give you that engagement ring."

Tonya laughed and said, "Those roses had better have shallow roots. If you really do make the Olympic team, you'll be all over the world for the next four years."

"That's true," Jon answered. "But my roots will be deep, and they'll be with you. I'm not a shallow man."

"I know that," Tonya said.

"We're young, but we're not shallow," Jon said. "That's what we have in common."

Tonya thought he was probably right about that.

Chapter 44

Marshall didn't know how to dance and he was pretty difficult to talk to but Lauren was glad she'd asked him. He did seem to like her a lot and it was good to have a date.

Once or twice she tried to talk with him about marine biology but he wasn't real good at talking about that, either. In fact, Marshall was a lot shyer than she was, Lauren decided.

She danced with Davey and Jon and talked to Jessica and Tonya mostly. At eleven, she realized she would have to kiss Marshall if she stuck around much longer and so she volunteered to wheel Cee Cee to her room, saying, "I want to ski one more time tomorrow morning so I need to turn in."

Marshall looked relieved and sad at the same time and she kissed him on the cheek as he walked her and Cee Cee to their room. Once inside the door, Cee Cee said, "That poor guy! I thought he was going to melt when you kissed him. He's so *gone* on you, it must hurt. I wish I had that effect on men."

Lauren wiped off the little lipstick she still had on and neatly folded up Cee Cee's skirt. "Thanks," she said. "I've never worn a mini before."

"You can have it," Cee Cee said. "From now on, I'm not wearing anything but blue."

"Poor Jessica," Cee Cee sighed. "She actually managed to look as if she were having fun."

Lauren knew that Cee Cee probably was still very tired from her ordeal of yesterday so she suggested they go right to sleep. Cee Cee talked a few minutes about Dr. Tucker but before long she began to snore lightly.

Lauren lay in the dark, wishing she could go to sleep so easily but knowing she was wide-awake. When the phone rang, she picked it up so quickly that Cee Cee just stirred lightly and rolled over.

The voice at the other end said, "Lauren?"

"Yes, this is Lauren."

"This is Greg. Are you still mad at me?"

"Oh, I don't know, Greg. What do you want?"

"Well, you're leaving tomorrow and I promised you a ride on the Sno-Cat, so I thought

I'd give it a try. Do you want to come for a ride with me?"

"Now?" Lauren asked. "It's eleven-thirty at night."

"It's New Year's Eve," Greg said. "If you don't have a date or anything, why don't you come? It's kind of fun."

It took Lauren just one minute to make up her mind. She said, "I'll be ready when you get here." She hung up and jumped out of bed, pulled on her long underwear, her heaviest and warmest snow clothing. She left a note for the girls, then ran out on the porch.

Greg parked the Sno-Cat in the yard and walked up to the porch. He stood under the porchlight, smiling up at her and he said, "I thought you'd say no. Why didn't you?"

"I'm not sure," Lauren admitted. "I couldn't sleep and I've never ridden in a Sno-Cat."

She followed him back to the huge machine and climbed on, exactly the way he showed her. Once she was up, inside the cab of the monstrous machine, she said, "It's a long way down."

"You're not scared, are you? I've seen you ski. I didn't think you'd be scared of anything."

"When did you see me ski?"

"Once by accident," Greg said. "The second time was this morning. I was going to talk to you but you ran off to break up your friend's romantic party. Why'd you do that?" He was laughing but he sounded curious.

Lauren blushed. "I didn't know they were kissing," she admitted. "I thought they fell down."

Greg laughed aloud and said, "I'll bet they were really glad you rescued them. What did Jon say?"

"He was nice. Do you know Jon?"

"Sure. My cousin is his coach. Works over at Mount Stowe."

"How many cousins do you have, Greg?"

"First, second, or third? Over a hundred for sure. My mom has five sisters and my dad has two sisters and three brothers. And they all have big families."

"They all sound so interesting," she said.

"Not all," Greg shook his head. "Jimmy's my cousin. I'm sorry about that whole mess, Lauren. I was stupid and macho."

"I think I overreacted," Lauren said thoughtfully. "I think I've been overreacting to a lot of things lately. Breaking up with Brian was hard on me and I've been scared."

"What was he like?"

"Brian? He was nice, I guess, and he was never afraid of anything. He called me Wren because I was so shy. But he liked me. At least I thought he liked me and then one day he liked Anne Pauling better."

"Hold on," Greg said and the Sno-Cat began to climb the long hill, grinding snow as it went up the steep slope.

Lauren's heart raced and she looked out the window at the snow below. "Does anyone ever turn over?" she asked.

"Not here," Greg answered, but he clearly needed to pay attention to what he was doing so Lauren was quiet until they got to the top of the hill.

They stayed on top for a moment and Greg said, "I think he was nuts to let you go."

"That's nice to hear." She smiled in the darkness. She did like Greg a lot. He wasn't as handsome as Jon or as talented as Davey or as smart as Dr. Tucker but . . . but he was nicer than Brian and he was smarter than Marshall.

"I'm glad you came out with me, Lauren," he said. "I know tomorrow's your last day, and I want us to part friends, not enemies. I really feel terrible about that whole thing."

Lauren said, "Let's just forget it. How often do you have to do this work?"

"I'm just a temporary," Greg answered. "They call my dad when they need extra help and if he's out of town, I take the job. My dad has three Sno-Cats and he farms them out for a living."

They started down the hill and this time, Lauren had to brace herself to keep from falling forward. She laughed and said, "This thing is like a giant snow-eating monster."

"You're right," Greg agreed. "I call her Gertie."

"Why do you think this awful-looking thing is female?" Lauren asked. She was really glad she'd come.

"Sexist, huh? My dad named her. Not me. I'm really not sexist at all."

"And I'm really not shy," Lauren teased.

"I don't think you're shy," Greg said. "I just think you're so beautiful that it's hard to get to know you. But you're the nicest person that I've met in a long, long time."

Lauren sighed and leaned back in the Sno-Cat and said, "You know what I like best about you, Greg?"

"No, what?" he answered.

"What I like about you best is that you don't talk all the time about how I look."

"Okay. I'll never mention your looks again," he promised solemnly. "I want you to like me, Lauren."

"I like people who know who I am," Lauren said. "You're relaxing to be around."

"Oh, I'm a relaxing kind of guy. Now hold on because we're going to go turn around."

In all, they went up and down the slopes twenty times and then Greg pronounced, "I guess I've done a good enough job so Dad won't fire me."

"Do you like this work?"

"It's not ski photography," Greg answered, "but it's kind of fun. I like being out in the night when no one else is around. Makes me feel special."

Lauren yawned and Greg said, "But I guess that's enough specialness for tonight. I'll take you back to the lodge." When they got there, he said, "Thanks, Lauren. It was a lot of fun having you along. I think you're a great sport."

"You are, too," Lauren answered. Then she looked at her watch and said, "It's three-thirty in the morning."

"Yeah," Greg answered, "too late for a New Year's Eve kiss, I suppose."

"No, I don't think so," Lauren answered. She turned and put her arms around his neck and kissed him swiftly and lightly on the lips, then jumped out of the Sno-Cat and said, "Thanks a lot."

Greg grinned at her and said, "I'll write to you, huh?"

Lauren waved and said, "Sure, that'll be

fine." Then she turned and ran into the lodge. When she got into the lodge, all three girls were sound asleep. She slipped in beside Jessica and was asleep herself in three minutes. In her dreams, she was riding in the Sno-Cat once again.

Chapter 45

Friday

Tonya couldn't wake Lauren in the morning and Jessica said she'd rather walk than ski so she ended up at the ski lift alone. She turned in everyone's equipment except hers and then went over to the lift where she found herself pushed onto a two-seater lift with Angel.

"I didn't think you could ski," Tonya said.

"I can," Angel said. "And my dad thinks I'm not getting enough exercise so here I am."

"And here I am," Tonya said dryly.

"I guess they're all still mad at me?" Angel asked in a very soft voice.

"Yeah, pretty much," Tonya said cheerfully.

"Are you mad, too?" Angel asked.

Tonya shrugged and said, "I don't really stay mad very often. Life's too short, and I'm a pretty easygoing person."

"Yes, you are. You know, you're nicer than the other girls."

"No, I'm not," Tonya answered. "It's just that you're not as jealous of me, so you're nicer to me. Haven't you figured that out?"

"I'm not jealous," answered Angel.

"Oh yeah? Then how come you've been giving Lauren and Jessica such a hard time this week?"

"I haven't been giving them a hard time," Angel said.

"Yes, you have, Angel. You have done just about everything you could to spoil our trip. If we'd called central casting and asked for a fly in the ointment we couldn't have done better."

"I'm not a fly in anybody's ointment," Angel said. "Jessica marched in here and took my boyfriend away from me."

"Jessica took nothing from you," Tonya answered. "Jessica found a guy who needed a friend because you were after him."

"You're not so nice. I've changed my mind," Angel said.

Tonya laughed and said, "I'm nice enough. I just want to try to make a point if I can. The point is — shape up. You're beautiful, you're rich, and you've got nothing to complain about, so why do you go around acting miserable?"

Angel turned and stared out over the valley.

"Nobody likes me. You're lucky, Tonya, everyone likes you."

"You still don't get it, do you? It isn't luck." Tonya jumped safely to the ground and laughed when Angel tried to make the same jump and tangled herself up and fell down.

A young man ran over and helped her up, asking, "Are you hurt?"

"You should have been here to help me," Angel said. "When my dad buys this place, he'll fire you."

"You'll never change, will you?" Tonya asked.

"I wouldn't know how to change if I wanted to," Angel said sullenly and looked out over the mountains.

"Well, I'll tell you how," Tonya offered. "Count your blessings every morning. Get up out of bed and make a list of the things that you're grateful for. Start out with your good looks. Add your money and your healthy body. Then go out and see others as real people. Not just as people who might have more than you do. Your trouble is, you treat people like they're not your equals. Either you think they're lower than you are or you're jealous of them."

They were at the top of the hill now. "I've got to go," Tonya said.

Angel said, "Thanks, Tonya, at least you talked to me. That's more than anyone else does."

Tonya laughed. "Take my advice and get real. Maybe then people will talk to you." Then she hugged Angel and said, "I don't think anyone really thanked you for saving Cee Cee's life yesterday. You did, you know."

Angel looked startled. "I guess I did."

"So that's good."

"Yes," Angel said thoughtfully, "that's good."

Jon was waiting for Tonya at the top of the hill, and he said, "I'm glad you came to say good-bye. What were you talking to Angel about?"

"I was giving her some good advice she probably won't take."

Jon shook his head and said, "Why would you bother to help Angel? I don't understand you."

"I'm just naturally helpful," Tonya laughed. She was quite cheerful and feeling glad to be alive despite the fact it was their last day.

"Why don't you help me figure out how to live without you for four months?" Jon asked and kissed her.

Tonya laughed, "I'll give you the same advice. Count your blessings every day."

He was nuzzling her neck and she pulled away, saying, "Your class is watching."

"Yeah," Jon agreed. "But if they ask me what I was doing, I'll just say I was counting my blessings. I'm going to miss you."

"I'm going now," she warned. "I don't want you to lose your job." She turned and skied away from Jon, not daring to look back.

She skied until an hour before the bus was to come for them and then she went back to the room where Cee Cee and Lauren were talking about their dates. "Do you think he'll write?" Cee Cee asked Tonya.

"Jon?"

"No. Of course Jon will write. I meant Greg."

"Greg?"

"Lauren went out with Greg last night after she left us. Very romantic ride on a Sno-Cat."

"That's nice," Tonya said. "Any word for Jessica?"

The girls faces fell and both shook their heads. "Still no answer at her home," Lauren said. "I don't know how she's standing it."

"Where is she? With Davey?"

"No," Lauren said. "She said she just wanted to be alone this morning. Poor thing. I feel so sorry for her."

Chapter 46

Jessica stood on the little stone bridge and looked out into the forest one more time. The birch trees seemed to have changed overnight into weeping willows. "Good-bye trees," she whispered. "You'll never be this beautiful to me again."

The tears formed in her eyes but she was so used to them by now, that she just brushed them away with her hand. Either she would be here again and the trees would seem more ordinary or she wouldn't ever be here again. Either way — the trees were special this morning.

A blackbird flew very close, lighting on a branch of one of the bare trees. Did that mean good or bad luck? She wasn't sure. Blackbirds could mean death, she decided, or they could simply mean that another forest creature was seeking food.

She could be dying and she was getting used to the idea or Davey could be right and she might be giving up hope too soon. She wasn't sure anymore. All she knew was that she loved this little bridge and she loved these bare trees and she loved life.

She smiled to herself. One thing's for sure. I've learned to appreciate life this week. She would tell that to Davey the next time she saw him, which she knew would be in about thirty minutes. She'd managed to sneak off to the woods alone but he would be there when she boarded the bus. She knew Davey well enough now to know he would be there, no matter what she'd said.

So she stood on the little bridge, remembering Davey's kisses and rehearsing what she would tell him about loving life when she saw him. She would tell him that the ordinary things were what were really important — things like the rough texture of this stone bridge and the way the blackbird darted between the branches like a zigzagging kite.

There was so much to say and so little time! And whatever time she had would be good. She was going to enjoy every moment of it. She would taste the mustard on the hamburger, smell the first spring flowers, and really pay attention to life. I'm going to be fully alive, she promised herself.

She turned and made her way back to the lodge, knowing they would all be there, waiting for her. If she knew Tonya, her bags would be on the ground, or already stowed on the bus. There wasn't anything else for her to do but say good-bye to those they were leaving behind and go home to whatever awaited her.

Sure enough, when she got to the lodge, the bus was already there, and the bus driver was packing their gear into the side of the bus. Tonya was supervising and Davey was standing there, looking worried.

"Hi," she said.

"Where were you?" Tonya demanded crossly. "I thought I was going to have to call an ambulance for him." She pointed to Davey.

Davey asked, "How did you manage to get away from me this morning? I looked for you in the coffee shop for breakfast and then all around."

"I'll miss you, Davey." She reached up and touched his face and said, "I'll call you right away."

"Why did you run away?"

"We had such a wonderful evening last night, I didn't want to spoil it by having you see me early in the morning." When Jessica saw the hurt look on his face, she kissed his cheek and said, "Davey, don't be like that. I just needed a little time alone. I have to face whatever I have to face alone, and I wanted to get ready for it."

Davey put his arm around her shoulder and said, "Jessica, you won't face whatever it is alone. I'll be with you. I'm with you all of the way. You know that now, don't you? Tell me you know that."

Jessica nodded her head and said, "Yes, Davey, I know that you're a good friend."

"More than a friend," Davey said. "I'm your good love."

Jessica smiled and said, "Yes, you are."

"We still don't know anything," Davey said. "Even if the diagnosis is not favorable, we still won't know. There's medical science, there're advances, there're lots of things that can be done. We must never give up hope."

Jessica nodded her head and looked gravely at Davey and said, "I promise you I will keep living until I draw my last breath. I promise you that whatever time I have ahead of me will be loving, quality time. And I promise you I will never give up." The tears that were rolling down both their cheeks were silent tears, and they held each other close, as though they would never leave each other.

As they pulled apart, Davey's voice was choked as he said, "Jessica, this has been a wonderful week for me."

"Me too, in spite of everything," Jessica answered. And then she said, "But Davey, I've got to get on the bus. They're all on now."

It was true. Everyone was on the bus except Jessica. The bus driver leaned over and growled, "You lovebirds going to stay here or go back to Connecticut with me?"

Jessica pulled away and said, "I'll call you as soon as I know for sure." It seemed as though she saw forever in Davey's eyes.

Just then, Marshall came running out of the lodge and said, "Here, take this." He shoved a piece of paper at Jessica and she nodded and put it in her pocket.

She stepped onto the bus and sat down beside Lauren. Jessica handed Lauren the paper and said, "I presume it's a love note from your bashful lover."

Lauren took the paper and started to crumple it up but Cee Cee grabbed it and began to unfold it. She intended to read it aloud but as her eyes looked down at the wadded-up paper, she said in amazement, "It's a telegram."

"Why would Marshall send Lauren a telegram?" Tonya asked. "He must really be crazy."

Jessica's heart began to beat rapidly. She remembered the beige envelope Marshall was carrying when Lauren asked him to the dance. That was yesterday morning. Was it possible the telegram was from her parents? That Marshall had forgotten to give it to her? Maybe it was good news! Maybe.

"It's not for her," Cee Cee said slowly.

"Is it for me?" Jessica asked softly. Cee Cee nodded and handed the telegram to her.

Jessica pulled the telegram from its envelope and looked down at the message.

> *Tried to reach you on the phone but your phones don't work. You are fine, totally fine. We are relieved and deliriously happy and have gone to the party. Love Mom and Dad.*

"I'm all right!" Jessica shouted.

They were all stunned except Cee Cee who threw her magazines up in the air and shouted, "Hip hip hooray! Hip hip hooray! Hip hip hooray!"

"You mean Marshall had this for twenty-four hours? How could he be such a jerk?" Tonya asked.

"It's all right," Jessica said. "I'm well! That's all that matters."

344

Jessica stood up and walked to the front of the bus. "Will you turn around?" she asked the driver. "I have some wonderful news to tell a friend."

"Can't." Then the driver looked at her and said, "The road is too narrow but you can call from Joe's Diner. I'll stop there. It will keep till we get to the bottom of the hill."

Yes, Jessica thought. It will keep another half hour.

The girls sat in the bus all holding hands tightly.

"This has been a *wonderful* week. Hasn't it?" Tonya asked.

"The best," Lauren said. "Next year we'll all do it again. Right?"

"Right!" the girls shouted together.

Point Romance

Caroline B. Cooney

The lives, loves and hopes of five young girls appear in a dazzling new mini series:

Anne – coming to terms with a terrible secret that has changed her whole life.

Kip – everyone's best friend, but no one's dream date...why can't she find the right guy?

Molly – out for revenge against the four girls she has always been jealous of...

Emily – whose secure and happy life is about to be threatened by disaster.

Beth Rose – dreaming of love but wondering if it will ever become a reality.

Follow the five through their last years of high school, in four brilliant titles: *Saturday Night, Last Dance, New Year's Eve,* and *Summer Nights*

A brand new series coming from Point...

Encounter worlds where men and women make hazardous voyages through space; where time travel is a reality and the fifth dimension a possibility; where the ultimate horror has already happened and mankind breaks through the barrier of technology...

Obernewtyn
Isobelle Carmody
A new breed of humans are born into a hostile world struggling back from the brink of apocalypse...

Random Factor
Jessica Palmer
Battle rages in space. War has been erased from earth and is now controlled by an all-powerful computer – until a random factor enters the system...

First Contact
Nigel Robinson
In 1992 mankind launched the search for extra-terrestial intelligence. Two hundred years later, someone responded...

Read Point SF and enter a new dimension...

P●INT CRiME

If you like Point Horror, you'll love Point Crime!

A murder has been committed . . . Whodunnit?
Was it the teacher, the schoolgirl, or the best friend? An exciting new series of crime novels, with tortuous plots and lots of suspects, designed to keep the reader guessing till the very last page.

School for Death
Peter Beere

Avenging Angel
Shoot the Teacher
David Belbin

Baa Baa Dead Sheep
Jill Bennett

Driven to Death
Anne Cassidy

Overkill
Alane Ferguson

The Smoking Gun
Malcolm Rose

Look out for:

Final Cut
David Belbin

A Dramatic Death
Margaret Bingley

Kiss of Death
Peter Beere

Death Penalty
Dennis Hamley